Wishin'
AND
Hopin'

Wally Lamb

HarperCollins*Publishers*

HarperCollins*Publishers*
77–85 Fulham Palace Road,
Hammersmith, London W6 8JB

www.harpercollins.co.uk

Published by HarperCollins*Publishers* 2009

A catalogue record for this book is
available from the British Library

ISBN: 978 0 00 735120 6

Printed and bound in Great Britain by
Clays Ltd, St Ives plc

Mixed Sources
Product group from well-managed
forests and other controlled sources
www.fsc.org Cert no. SW-COC-1806
© 1996 Forest Stewardship Council
FSC

FSC is a non-profit international organisation established
to promote the responsible management of the world's forests.
Products carrying the FSC label are independently certified
to assure consumers that they come from forests that are managed
to meet the social, economic and ecological needs
of present and future generations.

Find out more about HarperCollins and the environment at
www.harpercollins.co.uk/green

Wishin' and Hopin'

Wally Lamb is the author of three previous novels, most recently the *New York Times* bestseller *The Hour I First Believed*. His previous novels, *She's Come Undone* and *I Know This Much Is True*, were both number one *New York Times* bestsellers. He lives in Connecticut with his wife, Christine. The Lambs are the parents of three sons.

For Chris, a happier 1964.
And for my sisters (DNA-wise and otherwise) – Vita, Gail, Ethel.

Flight

The year I was a fifth-grade student at St. Aloysius Gonzaga Parochial School, our teacher, Sister Dymphna, had a nervous breakdown in front of our class. To this day I can hear Sister's screams and see her flailing attempts to shoo away the circling Prince of Darkness. I am, today, what most people would consider a responsible citizen. I have an advanced degree in Film Studies, a tenured professorship, and an eco-friendly Prius. I vote, volunteer at the soup kitchen, compost, floss.

A divorced dad, I remain on good terms with my ex-wife and have a close and loving relationship with our twenty-six-year-old daughter. That said, my conscience and I have unfinished business. What follows is both my confession and my act of contrition. Forgive me, reader, for I have sinned. It was I who, on that long-ago day, triggered Sister's meltdown. For this and all the sins of my past life, I am heartily sorry.

Lyndon Johnson was president back then, Cassius Clay was the heavyweight champ, and John, Paul, George, and Ringo were newly famous. Our family had a claim to fame, too. Well, *two* claims, actually. No, *three*. My mother had recently been notified that her recipe, "Shepherd's Pie Italiano," had catapulted her into the finals of that year's Pillsbury Bake-Off in the "main meal" category and she was going to be on television. I was going to be on TV, too— a guest, along with my fellow Junior Midshipmen on a local program, Channel 3's *The Ranger Andy Show*. So there were those two things, plus the fact that our third cousin on my father's side was a celebrity.

At the lunch counter my family ran inside the New London bus station, we displayed three posters of our famous relative that if, say, you were a customer enjoying your jelly doughnut or your baked Virginia ham on rye, you could, by swiveling your stool from left to right, follow the arc of our cousin's career. The black-and-white poster on the wall behind the cash register showed her in mouse ears and a short-sleeved sweater, the letters A-N-N-E-T-T-E spelled out across her flat front. In the poster taped to the front of the Frigidaire, she'd acquired secondary sex characteristics and moved on from TV to the movies, specifically Walt Disney's *The Shaggy Dog*, in which she had third billing behind Fred MacMurray and a half-human, half-canine Tommy Kirk. Poster number three, positioned over the fryolator and polka-dotted with grease spots, depicted our cousin in living color. Transistor radio to her ear, she wore a tower of teased hair and a white two-piece bathing suit, the top of which played peek-a-boo with what our dishwasher and part-time grill cook, Chino Molinaro, referred to as her "bodacious bazoom-booms." Alongside Frankie Avalon, Annette had by then become the lead actress of such films as *Beach Blanket Bingo* and *How to Stuff a Wild Bikini*, her celluloid star having ascended as her bra cup size worked its way through the alphabet. That's something that is much clearer to me today than it was when I was in fifth grade. Still, even back then, poster number three had already begun to set *something* atwitch in me, south of my navel and north of my knees.

I'm not making excuses here, but Sister Dymphna's emotional state was already fragile before that October afternoon, a scant six or seven weeks into the 1964–65 school year. My older sisters, Simone and Frances, had both survived tours of duty with "Dymphie," who, faculty-wise, was widely recognized as St. Aloysius G's weakest link. In Simone's year, she had yanked a kid's glasses off his face and snapped them in half. In Frances's year, she had turned her chair from her students to the blackboard and, elbows against the chalk tray, indulged in a crying jag that lasted all the way to the three o'clock bell. (Frances, who would later become a teacher, took it upon herself to stand and announce to her peers, "Class dismissed!") Sister Dymphna was thought of as moody rather than mentally ill— "high-strung" during her manic episodes, "down in the dumps" during her depressive ones. The latter mood swing was the preferred one, my sisters had assured me. When Dymphie got riled up, a heavy dictionary or a hooked blackboard pointer could become a dangerous weapon. But when she was depressed, she'd wheel the projector down from the office, thread it, and show movies while she sat slack-jawed and slumped at her desk, oblivious to bad behavior.

On the day Sister went crazy in front of us, she'd been mopey since morning prayers. We were therefore watching a double feature: before lunch, *The Bells of St. Mary's* with Ingrid Bergman and Bing Crosby in nun's habit and priest's cassock, and after lunch, *The Miracle of Marcelino*, a film about a pious homeless boy who is adopted by a community of monks. Lonny Flood and I hatched our plan in the cafeteria during what I guess you could call intermission.

Not unlike radio's Casey Kasem, Sister Dymphna rated my classmates and me each week from first to last based on our grades. She published a list at the far left of the blackboard and seated us accordingly, her smartest pupils in the first row from left to right, the academically middling students in the middle, and the slowest kids stuck in the back by the clanging radiators. Rosalie Twerski and I were, respectively and perennially, numbers one and two. My friend Lonny Flood usually found himself in the back row, often next to Franz Duzio. Lonny was both the tallest kid in our class and the oldest: a twelve-year-old double detainee whose sideburns and chin fuzz would become, by Easter vacation, shave-worthy. Conversely, I was the shortest and scrawniest fifth grader, counting boys *and* girls—a ten-year-old who, to my mortification, could have passed for seven. To make matters worse, with my big black eyes, up-slanting eyebrows, and mop of dark, curly hair, I bore a striking resemblance to Dondi, the adorable little Italian war orphan in the comic strips. On numerous occasions when I was down at the lunch counter, some new arrival would enter the bus depot, sit at a stool, and stare at me for a few seconds. We all knew what was coming next. "Say, you know who that kid kind of looks like?"

"Dondi!" Pop, Ma, Chino, and whichever of my sisters had drawn waitress duty that day would say it simultaneously.

Looking like a lovable little cartoon character was a double-edged sword. On the one hand, it made me vulnerable to my sisters' ridicule. On the other hand, my resemblance to Dondi—hey, even *I* had to concede that I was adorable—would frequently afford me the presumption of innocence when, more often than not, I was guilty. If, for example, Lonny Flood and I had stood shoulder to shoulder in some junior police lineup, I would most likely be the first suspect eliminated and Lonny the one fingered. "It's *him!*" the eyewitness might announce, pointing at Lonny, who kept a foil-wrapped Trojan hidden in the change pocket of his *Man from U.N.C.L.E.* wallet and who claimed to know the dirty words of the song "Louie, Louie."

And who, in fact, had brought the pocketful of BBs to school that day. Lonny and I conspired over half-pints of fruit punch and the lunch room's "turkey à la king with savory buttered rice." That said, neither of us had targeted the winged vermin that, an hour later, would cause such havoc and send Sister Dymphna on a temporary trip to "the funny farm." No, our intended victim, whose guts Lonny and I both hated, was the aforementioned Rosalie Twerski.

Rosalie was pig-tailed, hairy-legged, and insufferably obsequious—the kind of kid who, two minutes before the dismissal bell, might raise her hand

and ask, should the teacher have miraculously forgotten to assign a page of arithmetic problems or a dozen *Can You Answer These?* questions from our social studies book, "Do we have any homework tonight, Sister?" As I've mentioned, Rosalie's position at the top of the academic heap was a virtual lock, but nevertheless she was forever foraging for extra credit points she didn't really need. Her family was rich, or, as my mother used to put it, "la di da." The Twerskis' house on White Birch Boulevard had columns in front and a trampoline and a Shetland pony out back. Instead of clomping off the bus or hoofing it like the rest of us, Rosalie arrived at school every morning in her mother's maroon Chrysler Newport. Each year, she returned from Christmas vacation a week later than the rest of us, with a Florida tan and a bucket of stinky show-and-tell seashells that we had to pass from person to person during science. Her father owned a printing company, Twerski Impressions, which made Rosalie the recipient of an endless supply of the cardboard she was forever converting into the extra credit posters and placards with which our classroom was festooned. Suck-up that she was, she specialized in visual aids that lent themselves to the nuns' two favorite subjects, grammar and religion. In one such poster, the parts of speech were anthropomorphized: the active verb did push-ups, the passive verb sat and snoozed, the interjection slapped its hands against its cheeks, exclaiming, "Oh!" In another poster, cartoon letters "A" and "I" held hands like best friends or boyfriend and girlfriend. Said letter "A," "When two vowels go a-walking, the first one usually does the talking." "That's true," letter "I" agreed. "But remember, it's *I* before *E,* <u>except</u> after *C!!*"

On our first day in Sister Dymphna's class, Rosalie had arrived locked and loaded with a poster titled *Mortal Sinners: Burning in Hell or Headed There!* Below the Magic-Markered headline, she had scissored and glued magazine pictures of the damned and, beneath their images, had identified the transgressions that had cast them into Satan's lair: Lee Harvey Oswald and Jack Ruby (murder), Marilyn Monroe (suicide), Nikita Khrushchev (Communist), Rudi Gernreich (invented the topless bathing suit). Sister Dymphna loved Rosalie immediately and installed her as line leader, office courier, and our class's ambassador to the diocese-wide United Nations Day. So you couldn't really blame Lonny and me for putting BBs in our mouths and straws between our lips that afternoon as Sister, engulfed by a melancholy so profound that, as *The Miracle of Marcelino* unspooled, she did not even register that Pauline Papelbon was eating State Line potato chips right out of the bag, or that Monte Montoya and Susan Ekizian were playing Hangman instead of watching the movie, or that I had surreptitiously moved my seat to the back of the room for better positioning. By a prior agreement, Lonny and I had agreed to aim for the back of Rosalie's neck.

"Ow! Who did that?" she shouted when Lonny's very first BB hit its target dead-on. Heads swiveled from *Marcelino* to Rosalie, and then to Sister

Dymphna, who seemed not to have heard a thing. Lonny fired again, but this BB flew past Rosalie's left shoulder and ricocheted against the blackboard. His next one whizzed over her head and hit the movie screen. I somehow managed to inhale my first BB rather than propelling it forward, but coughed it right back up again—luckily, since the Heimlich maneuver had yet to be invented. On the screen, saintly little Marcelino was weeping for the poor. With my tongue, I repositioned the regurgitated BB, took a deep intake of breath, and raised my straw in preparation of a forward thrust. That's when it caught my eye: the little black blob nestled against the left side of the public address box.

Unsure of what I was aiming at, I fired and missed. Fired again and hit it. It moved. When my third BB also hit its mark, it emitted a high-pitched pinging sound. A wing unfolded. My fourth try was a miss, but my fifth was bull's-eye accurate. The bat skidded several inches along the wall, flapped its wings twice, and took flight. It soared from one side of the classroom to the other and then began circling the perimeter. It dipped and swooped between the projector and the screen, its shadow bisecting Marcelino's face in close-up. Alarmed, my classmates sprang from their seats, screaming, running for the door and the cloakroom. Arthur Coté raised the top of his desk, stuck his head inside, and let the top bang back down. Rosalie Twerski ripped one of her posters off the wall and curled it over her head like a tent.

The commotion awakened Sister Dymphna from her funk just as the bat zoomed across her field of vision, did a U-turn, and landed on her desk. The two faced off for a second or two. Then the bat opened its mouth, hissed menacingly, and took flight once more. That was when Sister began screaming about the devil. I was momentarily taken aback by this. I'd known that Bela Lugosi, Grandpa Munster, and other vampires could transform themselves into bats, but I'd not been aware that the Prince of Darkness could perform that particular parlor trick, too.

Then I remembered that Sister Dymphna was crazy and that the bat was probably just a bat.

Her shrieks were high-pitched and cringe-inducing, and I watched in horror as her flailing arms sent her statue of the Blessed Virgin teetering back and forth on its pedestal, then crashing to the floor where its head and torso parted company. "Satan, I rebuke you! Merciful Jesus, save these poor children!" To save herself, Sister dropped to the floor and crawled beneath her desk in an approximation of the duck-and-cover exercise we had practiced in the event that those evil atheists, the Soviets, ever dropped the bomb on the submarine base in nearby Groton—a despicable act of which, we were assured, Khrushchev was fully capable.

When Sister Dymphna's duck-and-cover defense dislodged her headgear, our class emitted a communal gasp. I had snuck back to my assigned seat by then and, from my vantage point (second desk, first row—the parochial school equivalent of a pricey orchestra seat), I had a better look than most at what was beneath. For years, Simone and Frances had had a running argument about what, exactly, the veils and wimples of nuns concealed. Simone swore "on a stack of Bibles" that these Brides of Christ shaved their heads as smooth and shiny as Yul Brynner's. Frances, the family skeptic, insisted just as adamantly that nunly baldness was nothing but a myth. Now I saw that both sisters had been half-right and half-wrong. De-wimpled, Sister Dymphna sported a stubbly salt-and-pepper buzz cut, the kind I got every first day of summer vacation.

It was the reliably pragmatic Kubiak twins, Ronald and Roland, who restored reason to room fourteen. The sons of a dairy farmer, they had both practical natures and experience with the multitude of bats that flew in and out of their barn on Bride Lake Road. While Roland threw open the classroom windows, Ronald walked calmly and purposefully to the supply closet, retrieved the broom, and began shooing. Grateful to be directed, I suppose, the frightened bat complied. It took a sharp right by the filing cabinet, sailed through the open window, and disappeared into the day. Everyone except Sister Dymphna took note that the crisis was over.

It took Mother Filomina, the principal, Mrs. Tewksbury, the office secretary, and Mr. Dombrowski, the school janitor, to coax Sister Dymphna out from under her desk and back onto her feet, all the while shushing her as she babbled a stream-of-consciousness cataloguing of her sins: she had coveted Sister Fabian's lavender soaps and pilfered all the butter creams out of Sister Scholastica's Whitman's Sampler; she had knowingly eaten half of a liverwurst sandwich on Friday and imagined what Father Hanrahan might look like naked. Mother Filomina, Mrs. Tewksbury, and Mr. Dombrowski closed ranks around Dymphie so as to protect her from us thirty-four incredulous eyewitnesses. Order was restored to Sister's habit and she was hurried out the door, down the stairs, and back over to the convent.

For the remainder of that afternoon, our class was demoted back to fourth grade where we doubled up with Sister Lucinda's class. "My students will practice their multiplication tables and Sister Dymphna's class will work on vocabulary," Sister Lucinda (a.k.a. "Juicy Lips Lu-Lu") decreed. "Who would like to go next door and get the workbooks?" Two hands shot into the air, mine and Rosalie Twerski's. "All right, Felix, you may go," Sister said. This was a small but rare victory; I was almost never chosen over the bane of my existence and chief competitor.

Standing at the threshhold of our evacuated classroom, I surveyed the chaos I had unleashed: spilled books and book bags, an overturned chair, the cock-eyed angle of Pope Paul's framed portrait, the decapitated Blessed Virgin. Up front on the pull-up portable movie screen, *The Miracle of Marcelino* played on. From the looks of it, the film had reached its climax. Marcelino's humble little bed was empty; the tearful monks, hands clasped in prayer, were looking skyward; and no lesser a deity than God the Father Himself was explaining (in voice over) why He had decided to croak the saintly waif and recall him back to heaven. I looked from the screen back to the empty corridor and, verifying that the coast was clear, entered our room. I turned on the lights, yanked the projector's electrical cord, and tiptoed over to my desk where I stuffed my pockets with incriminating evidence: BBs, cafeteria straws, the one-word note that Lonny Flood had passed me: "Now!" Then I gathered up the workbooks and walked back down the hall.

Sister Dymphna was absent for the rest of that week, and our substitute was Sister Mary Agrippina, a nasty all-purpose permanent substitute/enforcer nun who suffered neither fools nor funny business and maintained discipline by pinching the skin of a transgressor between her thumb and index finger, then twisting it. I should know; I had the black-and-blue marks to prove it. I'd been twistered twice, once for talking to my neighbor during silent reading and once for sticking a pencil stub between my nose and upper lip and pretending I was Hitler while Sister Mary Agrippina was talking about World War II.

I was philosophical about my bruises, though, figuring that Sister Mary Agrippina was my penance for having awakened the bat. Still, I was relieved when, at ten minutes to three on Friday afternoon, Mother Filomina came into our classroom to tell us that the following Monday we would meet our long-term sub—not a nun this time, but a lay teacher. "And Sister Dymphna will rejoin you all after Christmas vacation."

"*Lay* teacher," Lonny mused as we walked home together. "I guess that means all us boys are gonna get laid." I didn't know what that meant, exactly, but I could tell from the sound of Lonny's snicker that it was dirty.

"Yeah," I snickered back. "That'll be cool. Right?"

"Yeah. Hey, knock knock."

"Who's there?"

"Marmalade."

"Marmalade who?"

"Marmalade me. Who laid you?"

I dirty-snickered some more. "You're a pig," I said, hypothesizing that he'd just said something piggish.

Not long before this conversation, I had accompanied my pop during the morning doughnut run—we had a standing order for six dozen assorted from the Mama Mia Bakery, which we picked up every day at 5:00 A.M. before opening the lunch counter. "Hey, Pop, what's all this stuff about 'the birds and the bees?'" I'd asked, as nonchalantly as possible. He'd swallowed hard and taken a long time to respond, and when he finally did, he said, "Well, Felix, let's see now. I guess the first thing you oughta know is that, whenever you get a drink of water from a drinking fountain, you should never let your lip touch the metal. Because there are these diseases you can get, see?"

I *didn't* see, but by then we had pulled up to the bakery. "Be right back," Pop said and popped out of the car faster than a jack-in-the-box. Five minutes later, he was back with the six boxes, a chocolate doughnut for me, and a cruller for himself. "Here you go," he said. "Let's you and me stuff our faces." Halfway back to the bus depot, I figured out that stuffed faces couldn't ask or answer any more embarrassing questions. Pop's warning about drinking fountains would be both the beginning and the end of his sex education tutorial.

"A pig? Yeah?" Lonny said. "I know you are, but what am I?"

"A fuckhead," I said. Down at the lunch counter, Chino Molinaro was always calling someone a fuckhead when my mother wasn't around.

Lonny laughed. "I know you are, but what am I? Hey, by the way, Ding Dong, I bet you can't say this five times fast: I slit a sheet, a sheet I slit; upon a slitted sheet I sit."

"I can so."

"Yeah? Okay, let's hear you."

Had my mother heard my attempt, she would have whacked me a good one, the way she had when she overheard me, in imitation of Chino Molinaro, refer to Giants' quarterback Y.A. Tittle as "Y.A. *Tittie*."

On Monday, I smelled our new teacher before I saw her—and began immediately to sneeze. As she would do each day thereafter, she had doused herself with lily-of-the-valley perfume, a scent to which I discovered I was highly allergic. "*Bonjour, mes enfants*," she began. "*Je m'appelle Madame Marguerite Irène DuBois Frechette*, but you may call me, simply, Madame Marguerite. *Je suis enchantée* to make your acquaintance!" She had the kind of face that you'd expect to see gray hair on top of, but hers was a fiery red frizz. She was wearing a tight red sweater with a bow on one shoulder and high heels that you could see her painted toenails in and a straight black skirt—the kind my sisters, for some reason, called "pully skirts." She wore lots of big jewelry that made noise when she moved. Madame Marguerite was pretty exotic for St. Aloysius Gonzaga Parochial School.

"*Je suis* from Québec, Canada," she announced. (She pronounced it Cana-*DA*, not *CAN*-ada, and I remember thinking, sheesh, she comes from someplace that she doesn't even know how to pronounce?) I was busy holding a finger beneath my nose, trying to stifle another sneeze, when she asked who would like to go up to the world map and point to where Québec was located. I certainly *could* have done so; the year before, I'd placed second in the fourth grade geography bee. But of course, Rosalie Turdski had placed first, and now her hand shot up as I let go an explosive achoo.

"*Très bien, très bien*," Madame Marguerite said when Rosalie lifted the pointer off the chalk tray and pointed correctly to Québec. "And what, mademoiselle, might your name be?"

"*Je suis* Mademoiselle Ros*alie*," Twerski said, as if she, too, were French-Canadian, even though her mother had brought our class a pan of pierogi every single St. Joseph's Day since second grade.

"A-ah-ah-*choo!*" I said, with a force that probably could have registered on the Richter scale.

"God bless you, *mon petit chou*," Madame Marguerite said, turning to me. "*Comment vous appelez-vous?*"

I said the only thing I could think of. "Huh?"

"Heh heh heh heh," Madame said. "I asked you what your name is."

"Oh," I said. "Felix. . . . Funicello."

"Ah, *mais oui*," she said. "But you remind me of another *garçon Italien*—a nice little boy I read about in the newspaper every Sunday. And so I shall call you *Monsieur* Dondi!"

The whole class erupted in laughter: Rosalie, Arthur Coté, the Kubiak twins, even Lonny Fuckhead Flood. That was when I realized I'd been wrong before. Sister Mary Agrippina had not been my penance after all. Madame Marguerite was or, by Christmastime, would be.

2

French

I was seated at the far left end of the lunch counter, doing 360-degree spins on my stool and studying, kind of. *"La plume est sur la table. . . . La pluie est fine et persistante. . . . Mon parapluie est noir."* The week after her arrival at St. Aloysius, Madame Marguerite had reshuffled the seating chart; no longer were my classmates and I seated according to our academic rankings. Madame also reconfigured the fifth grade curriculum: less religion and long division to make room for the addition of conversational French.

It was a quiet evening down at the bus depot—a few travelers in the main hall waiting for the Shortline bus to Providence and a couple of sailors, just in on the Greyhound from New York, seated at the opposite end of the lunch counter eating cheeseburgers. None of our regulars were around: Spiro Sidoropolous, who ran the Elite Barbershop next door; or "Cowboy" Zupnik, the parking lot manager, with his fringed leather jacket, snakeskin boots, and yarmulke; or Cindy Creamcheese, the obese go-go girl who danced in a cage at the Hootenanny Hoot and always ordered the same thing: vanilla Coke, pepperoni omelet, and an Annette for dessert. (The Annette was my sister Simone's creation: a hot fudge sundae topped with two upright Oreo cookies— edible Mouseketeer ears.) Reverend Peavey, another regular, had stopped in earlier but hadn't stayed when there were no sailors for him to do his missionary work on. (I was well into my own adulthood when it finally dawned on me why all the adults back then made quotation marks with their fingers whenever they mentioned Reverend Peavey's "missionary work" with the young men of the U.S. Navy.) This drunk guy, Mush Moriarty, had been there earlier, too, but Chino'd told him he had to leave because he was sitting at a stool with his pants so droopy that you could kinda see the crack in his *culo*. (*Culo's* Italian for your rear end.) "Hey, Mush!" Chino had said to him, shaking his shoulder. "How am I supposed to sell ham sandwiches with your hams hanging out for all the world to see? You'll take away everyone's appetite."

"Mmph?" Mush had said, lifting his face off the counter. "Wudja say?"

Chino said he'd just told him to am-scray. "Yeah, okay, boss," Mush said, sliding off his stool and staggering away. One thing about Mush, Pop always said: When you told him to go, he went.

"Does Mush have a wife and live in a house and stuff?" I asked Chino.

"No wife as far as I know," he said. "Used to have one, maybe. He's got a room at that fleabag hotel on

Bank Street, last I heard. But he lives mostly inside the bottle these days." I thought I knew what Chino meant, but it made me think of that miniature U.S.S. *Nautilus* in the bottle that Pop made from a kit we got him last Christmas. (Pop used to be in the Navy, before there were nuclear submarines.) He keeps it on top of his dresser in his and Ma's bedroom. And I pictured Pop's same bottle, except instead of the *Nautilus*, a little shrunken Mush Moriarty in there going, "Help! I'm stuck! Get me out."

"*Madame Marguerite est Québecoise. . . . Je suis Américain.*" Grabbing on to the counter, I pushed off as hard as possible, closed my eyes, and began counting the number of rotations my stool would make before stopping: four, five, six, seven. The record I had to beat, set just minutes earlier, was nine. . . . *Je suis* getting very dizzy, I thought. *Je* hope I don't puke *sur la* counter.

Chino Molinaro called over to me. "Hey, 'Lix, what's that you're speaking down there? Pig Latin?"

I brought my stool to an abrupt stop, opened my

eyes, and rolled them at him. "It's *French*," I said, something any moron but him would know. "I'm doing my *home*work." Chino had once tried to justify to my sister Frances why he'd quit high school the day he turned sixteen: having seen a Gravy Train truck back up to the cafeteria, he refused to attend any school that fed its students dog food.

"French? Yeah? Well listen, Pepé LePew. Your old lady left me a note that I'm supposed to feed you supper cause they ain't getting back until around seven. So whataya want? French toast? Bottle of French dressing?"

"Hardy har har har," I said. "That was so funny, I forgot to laugh."

"Yeah, and maybe for dessert I can see if Ruthie Rottencrotch is around so's she can give you a French-kiss."

I wasn't sure what distinguished French-kissing from regular kissing, but in response, I made a face and rubbed the back of my hand across my mouth. Ruthie was another of our regulars—a cross-eyed "chicky boom-boom" (another of my sisters' terms) who'd recently been arrested for something called "lascivious carriage." I'd looked up "lascivious" in the dictionary—with some difficulty. That letter "c" in the middle had thrown me. *Exciting sexual desires*, it said. The "carriage" part was what was confusing; I couldn't imagine how a shopping cart from the First National could be used to do dirty stuff. Still, I wasn't about to ask Chino to explain. Pop's birds-and-the-bees tutorial might have come up short, but Chino's might be *too* informative. Sex was a subject I wanted to know more about but also (kind of) didn't.

"You know what?" I said. "In French, nouns are either male or female." High school drop-out or not, Chino was probably still educable, I figured.

He shrugged and said the same was true of American.

"*English*, you mean? No, it's not."

"Sure it is. The word *boobs* is female, right? And *jockstrap*'s male."

Or then again, maybe he *wasn't* educable. Sighing with exasperated tolerance, I glanced up at the menu board and told him I'd have a Sal's torpedo and a Suicide Coke.

"A Sal's and a Suicide. You got it, Frenchie."

My father's signature sandwich—ground chuck sautéed with onions and green peppers, simmered in tomato sauce, scooped onto a torpedo-shaped grinder roll and topped with provolone—was a nod to the nearby submarine base and a favorite of the "squids" taking buses out of "Rotten Groton" or returning to it. The Suicide Coke was Chino's invention: a fountain-drawn Coke mixed with squirts of lime, cherry, and strawberry syrups and topped with a scoop of vanilla ice cream and chocolate syrup.

I was at the lunch counter that evening because Pop had driven to the wholesaler's in Brooklyn and then was staying overnight at his friend Tootsie Cammarato's house in Queens. (Tootsie was my godfather—a cheapskate compared to Simone's and Frances's. My sisters both got money for Christmas and all's I ever got from Tootsie was a crappy box of ribbon candy that wasn't even mine; it was the whole family's, and plus I didn't even *like* ribbon candy.) My mother and sisters weren't around that night either; the three of them had taken the bus to Hartford to shop for outfits for Ma. The Pillsbury Bake-Off finals were fast approaching and Simone was insistent that no mother of hers was going to fly out to Hollywood and appear on national television wearing "old lady clothes." Frances, who was more interested in field hockey than fashion, had gone along for the ride and, most likely, to remind Simone how superficial she was. Having lost the argument with my parents about whether or not I was old enough to babysit myself, I'd been ordered to walk down to the bus depot after school so that Chino could watch me. "*Chino?*" I'd gasped. "Why don't you just hire Odd Job to babysit me!" Pop, Ma, and I had seen *Goldfinger* at the drive-in that summer and Ma had later reported that she'd had a dream in which Odd Job was chasing her, so I thought mine was a clever argument. My parents sure didn't. Ma just laughed and Pop said he was pretty sure that the closest thing Chino got to deadly jujitsu moves was slapping on Hai Karate aftershave.

"Hey, you want fries with your torpedo?" Chino asked. "They're *French*."

I got off my stool and went behind the counter. "*I'll* make them."

"Yeah? Does your father let you use the fryolator now?" I lied and said he did. "Okay, then. But first, why don't you go play us some tunes? Here, catch." He tossed me a quarter. "And while you're at it, ask those two if they want anything else, will ya?" He pointed his chin at the sailors at stools fifteen and sixteen. This was cool, at least. My parents insisted I was too young to wait on customers, which I wasn't. And luckily, I was still wearing my St. Aloysius uniform—navy blue pants, powder blue shirt (minus the "fruit loop" that Geraldine Balchunas had pulled off of it, even though girls pulling fruit loops off the boy's uniform shirts is forbidden), and red clip-on tie—outfitted, as far as I was concerned, like a waiter at a fancy restaurant. But first things first.

The records in the lunch counter's jukebox got changed every other week by this guy named Manny. Mostly, our customers wanted to hear Motown or British Invasion. My sister Frances had grown particularly fond of the British pop star Dusty Springfield, and Manny accommodated her with Dusty's 45s—"I Only Want to Be with You," "Wishin' and Hopin'"—which Frances played over and over when she was down at the lunch counter helping Pop. But Manny knew better than to pull any of the 45s that featured our cousin's three biggest hits, "Tall Paul," "O Dio Mio," and "Pineapple Princess," which, everyone in our family knew, thanks to Simone, had reached as high as numbers 7, 10, and 11, respectively, on the Billboard Hot 100 chart. I dropped the coin into the slot and pushed the buttons I knew by heart: A-5, C-11, and E-8.

Chalk on the sidewalk
Writin' on the wall
Everyone know it
I love Paul

I went behind the counter again and walked jauntily toward the sailors. "Can I get you anchor clankers anything else?" I'd heard Simone say that sailors were the best tippers, especially when you teased them a little, but these guys looked more bugged than amused.

"Geeze, I don't know, Short Stuff," the not-pimply one said. "What do you got for dessert?" I told him I recommended the Annette sundae.

"Jesus H. Christ," the other one said. "They got her on the walls, on the jukebox. They even got a goddamned sundae named after her. This place has fuckin' Funicello fever."

I pursed my lips. "She happens to be our *cousin*," I said.

Neither seemed to register the significance of what I'd just told them. "Gimme a slice of banana cream pie," Pimple Puss said. His friend said all's he wanted was a glass of water and a toothpick.

I got their stuff and placed it on the counter in front of them. "Oh, by the way," I said. "Just in case you didn't know, I'm in Junior Midshipmen and we're gonna be on this TV show called *Ranger Andy*. And this coming spring, we're going on a field trip to New Bedford and sleeping overnight. On a *ship*."

"Wow! He's gonna sleep on a *ship!*" Mr. Not Pimples said. "That sounds real thrilling. Don't it, Marty?"

"Yeah. Whoop-de-do. Wish *we* could sleep on a ship sometime."

I thought suddenly of Lonny Flood—how much better he'd be at conversing with these guys. Then I thought of Lonny's tongue-twister. "Hey, can you say this five times fast?" I asked, then messed it up. "I slit a sheet, a sleet I shit, upon a shitted sleet I shlit."

The goons guffawed. "Hey, pal!" one of them called over to Chino. "Is your waiter here a kid or a fuckin' midget?"

"Let's put it this way," Chino said, approaching.

"He just moved here from Munchkinland." The three of them cracked up.

"That's about as funny as crippled kids!" I said.

Blinking back tears, I walked to the other side of the lunch counter, sat, and turned my back to them. But instead of feeling bad about having hurt my feelings, they started telling these jokes I didn't even get. "Took my girl to a game at Fenway last week," Chino said. "I kissed her between the strikes and she kissed me between the balls." Yeah, like *he* had a girlfriend. That time he called our house and asked to speak to Simone, she'd pantomimed gagging and scrawled me a note: *Tell him I have the flu.* But I'd had a better idea and told Chino, instead, that if he was calling to ask my sister out on a date, he'd better not because it would make Ma so mad, she'd probably have my father fire him. Officially, Pop was Chino's boss, but Ma was the one he was afraid of; I'd once overheard him refer to her as "a real gonad cruncher," and whatever that meant, I was pretty sure it wasn't a compliment.

"How is a woman like an oven?" one of the squids asked.

"Beats me," Chino said. I could hear the grin in his voice. "How?"

"Because you gotta heat it up before you stick the meatloaf in."

Man, they all loved that one! Their stupid laughing all but drowned out Annette's double-track singing. *Tall Paul, tall Paul, tall Paul, he's my all.*

After the sailors left, I ate my torpedo and drank my Suicide Coke. "Hey, 'Lix," Chino said. "Don't let what those two squids said bother you. They're just a coupla fuckheads, that's all."

I closed my eyes, rotating on my stool and mumbling it so that he could barely hear me. "Takes one to know one." Instead of getting mad like I kinda hoped he would, he just laughed.

In the silence that followed, I watched him wipe the coffee mugs he'd just washed and stack them in a pyramid. Looked down at the mimeographed sheet of words we were supposed to practice. "What *is* French-kissing, anyways?" I said. Chino placed a mug at the apex of his pyramid. He said it was like regular kissing, only the guy stuck his tongue inside the girl's mouth. And if he got lucky, she'd stick her tongue inside his mouth, too. "Yecch," I said.

"Well, Felix, don't knock it until you try it. You know—*years* from now, I mean. And don't tell your mother I told you."

I looked at the big clock out in the depot. Looked back at my stupid French. *"Je m'appelle Felix. Comment vous appelez-vous?"* Why had those big fat liars said they'd be home by seven o'clock if they didn't mean it? All's I wanted to do was go home.

"Hey! Yoo hoo," Chino said. "What do you say? Can you?"

"Can I what?"

"Hold down the fort here for a few minutes so's I can go take a leak?" I nodded and he headed for the restrooms on the other side of the depot.

While he was gone, I realized I'd forgotten to

make my French fries. I grabbed the basket, walked over to the fridge, and took two fistfuls from the freezer. Back at the fryolator, I lowered the basket of icy potato strips into the molten lard. When I looked up from the sizzle, there was Annette in her white bathing suit, smiling at me, eye to eye. I looked over my left shoulder, my right. All the benches in the hall were empty. The ticket guy was dozing in his cage. Should I? Shouldn't I? I climbed up onto the counter, leaned to my left, and poked my tongue out a little, touching it to Annette's paper mouth. French-kissing my cousin's poster felt kind of stupid but kind of exciting, too. I did it again.

At which point, I heard a loud pop and felt hot grease hit my neck. "Ow!" I yelled, the way Rosalie Twerski had when Lonny's BB hit her. Grabbing onto my throat, I dislodged my clip-on tie, and it fell into the fryolator. I stood there, watching it sizzle and sink.

✳　✳　✳

When Ma, Simone, and Frances got off the bus from Hartford, they were carrying boxes and garment bags and talking a blue streak. It was closer to eight o'clock than seven. "How come you're so *late*?" I demanded.

"It took longer because Ma got her hair styled," Frances said.

"At a salon!" Simone added. "And she got four new outfits. Doesn't her hair look cool? Look how much younger she looks!"

At which point I really noticed my mother. Her regular hair had been poufed up into a tall beehive style with a big swirling curl on one side and a French twist in back. Her head looked like a giant Dairy Queen.

"Hey, Mrs. F," Chino called over. "Va-va-voom." Ma waved him away with her hand and said okay, okay, that was enough of that. But for once, she was smiling at Chino instead of frowning at him.

"Felix, check out her skort," Simone said.

"Her what?"

"Her skort. They're *real* popular now. Real *modern*. Ma, turn around."

My mother did as she was told, as if the trip to Hartford had turned her into a zombie or something. She was wearing a skirt in front and Bermuda shorts in back and you could see her veiny legs either way.

"Well, Felix, what do *you* think of my new look?" Ma asked timidly.

I shrugged and looked away. "How should I know?"

Her smile twitched a little. "Do you think Daddy will like it?"

"Don't ask me. Ask him." What did she have to keep looking at me for? I was *my* same self. She was the one who was different. I was wishing she hadn't even entered her stupid Pillsbury Bake-Off.

"How did you make out today, sweetie?" she asked. "How was school?"

Instead of answering her, I asked a question of my own. "How come your legs look like blue cheese?"

Ma turned immediately to Simone. "See! I told

you this was too short." Simone said it wasn't—that I was just being a little jerk.

"As usual," Frances added.

Ma turned back to me. "What did you have for supper, honey?"

Nothing, I told her. Just a Suicide Coke. "And by the way, I hope you know you have to buy me a new uniform."

"A new—"

"I could have gotten killed, you know. While you were out doing all your shopping."

"Gotten killed? What do you mean?"

"Boiled in oil!" Ma and Simone exchanged confused looks, but Frances made some smart remark about Kentucky Fried Felix. "Oh yeah, Frances the Talking Mule, real funny!" I stuck my tongue out at her, too. Ma *hated* it when I did that, same as she did when I blew bubbles in my milk with a straw.

"Cool it there, Dondi," Chino said, approaching us. And to Ma, "He just had a little accident, Mrs. F. That's all."

"A *little* accident?" I countered. Like Perry Mason, I walked behind the counter and pointed to Exhibit A: my ruined red clip-on tie, resting atop a bed of greasy paper towels. I looked from my alarmed mother to Annette on the wall above the fryolator, smiling her placid paper smile, listening to her transistor radio. Then I turned back to Ma. I had intended to glare at her but, instead, began to cry.

"I fried my tie," I said.

My sisters burst into peals of laughter.

3

Confession

Tons of stuff was *already* happening that week. Saturday was Halloween. (Lonny and I were trick-or-treating in my neighborhood, and then he was sleeping over.) On Tuesday, our school was having our mock election, plus it was the day of the real election and either we'd have our same president still (LBJ) or else Barry Goldwater (AuH_2O), who was from Arizona. On Thursday, Ma was leaving for California, which, on the map, was right next to Arizona, which, if you drove from there through

New Mexico, you'd be in Texas where President Johnson was from. And now, sheesh, on top of everything else, Madame had just told us that our class was getting a new student—a girl who had moved here, not just from some place close like Rhode Island but from a *foreign country*!

Evgeniya (Zhenya) Vladimirovna Kabakova

Madame turned away from the name she'd just written on the board and smiled. Could anyone guess from her name which country Zhenya came from?

Rosalie's hand went up. "Poland?" Madame shook her head.

I put my hand up next. Figuring "Kabakova" sounded kind of like "capicola," I guessed Italy. Madame said, "No, heh heh heh, Zhenya is not *une jeune fille italienne.*"

MaryAnn Haywood guessed Ireland, Arthur Coté Japan. Eugene Bowen thought either Africa or South America. *"Non, non, et non,"* Madame said.

"Zhenya is *une jeune fille russe*—a Russian girl. She and her family have moved here from the Soviet Union." My classmates and I looked at each other, aghast. Rosalie's hand shot back up and Madame nodded.

"Is she a Communist?"

Madame frowned a little and shrugged, palms out. "Perhaps *oui*, perhaps *non*. Whatever she is, we shall show her what a friendly class we are when she arrives. *N'est-ce pas?* A few of us nodded cautiously; most remained noncommittal. "*Et bien.* Now please take out your copies of *The Yearling* and read the next chapter *en silence* until we are called over."

Called over to Final Friday confessions, Madame meant. On the last Friday of each month, St. Aloysius Gonzaga students in grades three through eight went next door, class by class, to come clean about their sins and receive penance and absolution.

Final Fridays were kinda good and kinda bad. Yes, you got out of doing work for an hour or so, but only so you could go to church. It was a far cry from a field trip to the Peabody Museum, say, where there were dinosaurs, or to Channel 3 in Hartford, where we were going next month in Junior Midshipmen so's we could be on *Ranger Andy*. Final Fridays could be good or bad, too, depending on who you got for a priest. It could either be Father Hanrahan, who gave cinchy penances (and who rode a motorcycle and could make outside shots on the basketball court, plus he liked the Beatles)—or Monsignor Muldoon, who was about 500 years old and kind of like Phineas T. Bluster, Crabby Appleton, and clueless Mister Magoo, all rolled into one.

I opened my copy of *The Yearling*. In the chapter we'd read the day before, Jody's father Penny had survived his rattlesnake bite. The problem—the "conflict," it was called—was that the deer Jody's father had had to kill to make the poultice that drew out the venom and saved his life had been a *mother* deer. A doe. So now her fawn was an orphan. I knew that Jody was going to adopt it for a pet and name it Flag because I'd peeked at some of the later chapters, even though we weren't supposed to read ahead, and if we did anyways, we were supposed to keep what happened to ourselves and not tell our neighbors. . . . In my opinion, silent reading kinda stunk because, even though I was the second smartest kid in our class, everyone around me read faster than me, even Lonny, except he was probably skipping paragraphs or even whole pages. . . .

The wall clock's minute hand reared back, then lunged forward with an audible *ca-chunk*. . . .

The thing I didn't get was how, first we had to practice our duck-and-cover exercises all last year because the Soviet Union was our enemy and now we were going to have a girl from there right in our class, and we were going to have to be nice to her, and I didn't know if anyone else had thought about this, but maybe she was a *spy*. . . .

The P.A. box *click-clicked*. "The sixth graders may now pass," Mother Filomina's voice said. *Click.* That was the way they called us over to confession: they started with the eighth graders and counted backwards, which meant, if sixth grade was going, then our grade was getting called next. Soon, I hoped, because silent reading was so *boring.* . . .

You know what would be cool? If, the day God the Father came back to earth for Judgment Day, it was just his voice on every single P.A. in the whole wide world. Except then, how could poor people in places like China and Africa hear him, because there probably weren't many P.A.s there, right? . . .

Ca-chunk.

Earlier that day? You know what Madame Marguerite told us? That from now on, we couldn't call her Madame Marguerite anymore. Now we had to call her Madame Frechette, or simply Madame. All the other kids had looked at each other like *huh?* I was the only one who knew what was going on. Madame was working on her "needs improvement"s. . . .

I had a pet once, two Easters ago. Not a fawn like Flag or some big-shotty pet like Rosalie's stupid Shetland pony, Ginger Gal, that she's always bragging about. My pet was this little baby chick we got at Thompson's Feed and Grain store. It was purple, on account of they dyed all the chicks for Easter. Popeye, I named him, because I liked Popeye cartoons and because he kind of had these poppy-outy black eyes. He got sick after about a week and started losing his balance and closing his eyes. (I hadn't realized before that chickens had eyelids.) Then he kind of curled up in a corner of the shoebox I was keeping him in and, at night while I was sleeping, he croaked. Frances and I buried him in our backyard, near where Ma's rose bushes are—or, as Pop called Ma's rose bushes, her restaurant for Japanese beetles. I made a cross for Popeye out of two popsicle sticks and some glue and stuck it on top of his grave, and then Frances and I said the Our Father. I asked Fran if she thought there was a different Heaven for animals, and she said, how should she know because, first of all, she wasn't an animal and second, she'd never been dead.

Ca-chunk.

When were they going to call us fifth graders over there? Next *year*? Not that I really wanted to go over, with what *I* had to confess. Oscar Landry's already on page 42 and all's I'm on is page 37. There's an illustration on page 40 and Oscar's way past that and I won't even get to it until three more pages. . . .

After Popeye died, I didn't even *want* any other pets because I was sad. And I was kind of sad and kind of glad that Ma was going on her California trip. Sad because she had never gone away before and I was probably going to miss her, but glad because Pop said if Ma won the grand prize, we could buy a brand new car, either a Cadillac or a Buick Riviera, and it was going to have air-conditioning, no matter which one we got. I was hoping we'd get the Riviera because the '65s had concealed headlights that you could only see when you put the headlights on, and when you turned them off again, these doors came down over them, kind of like eyelids. Me and Pop and Frances seen one in the showroom at Broadway Buick and the guy demonstrated the headlights for us. Royal Blue, the showroom Riviera was, which was the color I wanted. Fran wanted Country Club

Red. Pop said Ma would be the one who got to pick the color out because—

Click, click. "The fifth graders may now pass." *Click.*

Before any of us kids could stand up, Madame sprang from her seat, clapping her hands. *"Dépêchez-vous, mes enfants!* No dawdling, now. Hurry, hurry!" Everyone was looking at each other, wondering why she was having a nervous breakdown about us going over to the church, but once again, I knew that it was because of her "needs improvement"s.

And you know how I knew? Because the day before, out on the playground at recess, Ronald Kubiak had fired the dodge ball and hit me on the shoulder, tagging me out third to last. (In dodge ball, the Kubiak twins always started the game as "ends" and often kept those positions until recess was over.) As I waited on the sideline to see if Rosalie or Johnny Bartlett would survive or get nailed by a Kubiak, Madame had approached me. Would I please be *un bon garçon* and run up to our room and fetch her sunglasses, heh heh heh? (That was one of the weird things about Madame: she was always chuckling at things that weren't funny.) "*Oui*, Madame," I'd said, aware that Rosalie was watching us when she should have been watching out for the dodge ball, because Roland Kubiak fired it at her and got her in the small of her back, which threw Johnny into "sudden death." Rosalie started crabbing that it wasn't fair because she hadn't been ready yet. But she *would* have been ready if she wasn't always minding everyone else's business.

Back in the building, I'd mounted the staircases and, at the water fountain on our floor, had treated myself to a long, relaxing drink. (With Pop's warning whispering in my ears, I took care, of course, to avoid contact with the spout.) The opportunity to get an extra drink had been planned but the opportunity to snoop around Madame's desk hadn't been. I just did it without thinking about it first, so it was probably a venial, not a mortal, sin. (Sins that you plan out are worse than sins you just do without thinking about it first.)

Madame's grade book lay open on her blotter. Since she'd discontinued Sister Dymphna's practice of publicly ranking each of us on the left end of the blackboard, I decided to check out the current standings. Rosalie still had the longest string of check-plusses, big surprise, and I was still in second place. But from the look of it, both Oscar L. and MaryAnn H. were closing in on me. Lonny's check-minuses had put him in dead last place.

Madame's top left desk drawer held a collection of stuff that she, and Sister Dymphna before her, had confiscated: a kind of graveyard for squirt guns, wax lips, Lonny's whoopee cushion, et cetera. There was a Beatles magazine in there, a *Jughead* comic book, a "Watermelon Pink" lipstick, some packs of Wacky Plaques. And tons of candy: Mounds, Milky Ways, a Sky Bar, a box of malted milk balls. All of the above, plus enough packs of gum to fill the rack down at the lunch counter. I reclaimed the Juicy Fruit I'd lost the week before. "Gum, *monsieur?*" Madame had asked, one eyebrow raised. "Or are you chewing your cud?

Heh heh heh." I grabbed the whoopee cushion, too, and hid it in my social studies book, figuring I'd give it back to Lonny once we were safely off school property. I was being a little like Robin Hood, I figured.

Peering into Madame's open pocketbook (and shaking it a little), I'd spotted a pink wallet, a pack of brown cigarettes called Gauloises, some keys on a key chain, and two bottles of perfume: that lily-of-the-valley stuff that made me sneeze whenever Madame roamed the aisles to check our seatwork, plus a second kind of perfume called "cognac."

Recalling my official mission, I'd grabbed Madame's sunglasses and turned to go back outside, but then had done an abrupt about-face, curious to check out something I'd seen out of the corner of my eye: a sheet of paper turned face down on Madame's desk, on the back of which she'd scrawled, in red correcting pencil, *Merde!* On the bus the day before, a seventh grader named Jacques Lavoisseur had taught Lonny and me some French words that were never going to show up on any of Madame's mimeographed sheets. I'd forgotten most of them, but for some reason remembered that *merde* meant shit. I flipped the paper over.

From what I could figure out, it was some kind of report card for teachers. It had three categories with typed comments under each. Mother Filomina's signature was at the bottom.

SATISFACTORY

1. Rapport with students seems generally positive.

2. Bulletin boards are educational and neatly organized. I especially liked your display of the upcoming presidential election. You should note, however, that it is Electoral College, not Collage. Please correct.

1. Students should refer to you by your sur-
   name, not your given name, as this more
   formal appellation is more respectful and
   will result in fewer discipline problems.
   Speaking of which, were you aware that
   several of the children were passing notes
   during your arithmetic lesson, and that
   Pauline Papelbon was surreptitiously sucking
   on a Sugar Daddy before I gave her a sharp
   look?

2. Fifth grade students should be assigned 60 to
   90 minutes of homework per night. Playing
   outside so as to experience the joy of the nat-
   ural world should <u>not</u> be considered homework. (I have received calls from parents.)

3. Please try to dress as demurely as possible.
   Open-toed high heels and seamed fishnet

stockings, for example, are not appropriate for a parochial school environment.

4. You must work on delivering your class more promptly to the cafeteria at lunchtime and to their "extras"—gym, music, assemblies, Final Friday confessions, etc.

ADDITIONAL COMMENTS

I. While I have no strong objection to your acquainting the children with the French language, you must remember that this instruction falls under the category of "enrichment" and should <u>not</u> supersede academics and/or religious instruction. You might also wish to emphasize French culture, in particular the fact that France is a Roman Catholic country from which many saints have hailed. These include, of course,

Joan of Arc as well as Martin of Tours, and Teresa of Lisieux ("the Little Flower").

2. I appreciate your having volunteered to stage a series of costumed *"tableaux vivants"* for this year's Christmas program, given your experience with theatricals, and I will certainly consider and discuss with the rest of the faculty in the coming weeks. However, you should know that our Christmas program is well established, and that the audience who attends annually has certain expectations as to the format. They might not embrace the sort of pageantry you propose.

> *Very truly yours,*
> *Mother M. Filomina, Principal*

Reading Mother Fil's comments, I felt sorta sorry for poor Madame. Sure, she was weird, but she meant well. And compared to Sister Dymphna, she had way more of what Pop called "zippity-doo-da." But Madame's report card read kind of like a teacher's version of Lonny Flood's. I didn't know what "vivants" meant, but I figured *"tableau"* was French for "table." I didn't get why Madame was volunteering to put a costume on a table, unless, maybe, a *"tableau vivant"* was like a French tablecloth.

No dawdling now! Line up! *Dépêchez-vous!"* she pleaded. Yup, she was definitely working on her "needs improvement"'s.

I got in line by the back door and Marion Pemberton cut in front of me. Marion's a boy, not a girl, even though he has a girl's name, which, in a way, is worse than having everyone call you Dondi. Marion's the only colored kid in our grade. Black, I mean. At Sunday dinner last Sunday, Pop started telling us about, the day before, this sailor was sitting at the lunch counter having a tuna salad sandwich and a Fresca? And Pop could tell he was from the South because he had a Southern drool, which is an accent like that creepy little girl on the Shake 'N Bake commercial who, when her father comes home and says, "What's for dinner?" and the girl goes, "Mama made Shak'n'Bake and ah hailped." But anyways, Pop said, "And then this colored guy comes over and sits down at the stool next to him, and the Southern guy gets up and moves two stools down, as if the colored guy—" And Frances interrupted him and said, "What color was he?" And Pop went, "Huh?" And Frances said, "Was he green? Yellow? Purple?" Then she told us that her civics teacher told her class that, from now on, colored people didn't want to be called "colored" or "Negro"; they wanted to be called either "black" or "Afro-American." And Pop rolled his eyes and went, "Well, excuse me, Martin Luther King's secretary, but do you mind if I finish telling my story now?" But anyways, when Marion Pemberton cut me in line, I said, "Hey! No cuts, no butts, no coconuts." And he looked back at me and smiled and shook his finger in my face and said, "Wait'll the NAACP hears about *this!*" And I elbowed him in the back. (But we were just kidding. Marion and me are friends. One time, he and his mother were at the bus station picking up one of their relatives who was coming in on the New York bus and Pop let me make Marion a free float—orange soda with vanilla ice cream.) Marion's always saying that for a joke: "Wait'll the NAACP hears about *this!*" Like when he doesn't get picked right away in dodge ball, or when he wants to trade you something in his lunch for something in yours and you say no. NAACP means National Association for the something of Colored People. I mean *black* people. Except why don't they call it the N.A.A.B.P.?

Exiting the classroom, the thirty-four of us clomped in thunderous silence down the two flights of stairs and out the front door. With Madame clucking and clapping behind us, we slogged past the holly bush we'd planted for all the poor kids around the world who weren't lucky enough to live in a democracy. We passed the statue of Martin de Porres, the Afro-American saint from Peru or someplace who, Sister Dymphna told us, used to *glow* when he prayed and could be in two places at once, and could communicate with animals using ESP. We ambled past the Blessed Virgin's grotto where, each May, an eighth grade girl was chosen to dress in a bride's gown and veil, climb the step stool, and put a crown of flowers on Mary's head. (Simone had been chosen as the bride in her year; Frances had not been in hers but had insisted she wouldn't have done it, even if she *had* been picked over Bryce Bongiovanni, who was a brown-noser at school but a chicky boom-boom *out of* school, and who, Frances knew for a *fact*, had shoplifted at Rosenblatt's Clothiers and made out in the indoor show with "Jesse" James Bocheko.) My classmates and me rounded the corner, made the sign of the cross, and mounted the church steps, accompanied by Madame's *"Dépêchez-vous! Dépêchez-vous!"* And I was like, jeeze, all right already, re*lax*.

Inside, we faced a vestibule inspection conducted by the aforementioned skin-twister, Sister Mary

Agrippina. We boys were lined up, eyeballed, and ordered to tuck in our shirts, check our zippers and shoe laces, and, if necessary, spit onto our hands and pat down our cowlicks. Girls who had forgotten to bring a hat or mantilla to school that day were assigned detention and ordered to cover their heads with bobby-pinned sheets from Sister M.A.'s roll of paper towels—or, if a girl happened to be wearing a cardigan sweater over her St. Aloysius Gonzaga uniform, she could put her sweater on her head and button it beneath her chin. Two Final Fridays ago, I had noted to one sweaterhead, MaryAnn Vocatura, that with her sleeves drooping down the sides of her face, she looked like a basset hound. MaryAnn's response had been reasonable enough, I thought; she'd socked me in the arm. But Rosalie, whose business it *wasn't*, had ratted me out to Sister Mary Agrippina, who, in turn, had grabbed the back of my neck and squeezed hard, dropping me to my knees on the vestibule floor.

Declared acceptable, we fifth graders were given the go-ahead to enter the church proper, where we were met by St. Aloysius's vice-principal and Final Friday traffic cop, Sister Fabian—not to be confused with Sister Elvis, Sister Ricky Nelson, or Sister Bobby Rydell, this being a standard joke among the St. Aloysius student body. "You to the right," Sister Fabian decreed. "You to the left. Right. Left. Right. Left." Confession, absolution, and penance under these circumstances was, as Pop would say, a crap shoot. That morning my luck was crappy. I got Monsignor Muldoon.

"You're next, Felix! Get the lead out! Let's go!" Sister Fabian ordered, loudly enough to be heard by the angels in heaven, let alone by my father-confessor. Reluctantly, I detached myself from the boys' line and approached the confession box. I parted the curtain, entered, and knelt.

Like a life-sized shadow puppet, Monsignor shifted behind the confessional screen. I waited while he unwrapped a Life Saver and popped it in his mouth. Butter rum, the same flavor my father liked; I could smell it through the gray-silk screen that separated us. For a month or more during morning exercises, our class had been asking God to help Monsignor break his smoking habit. Doctors' orders: emphysema. I heard the crunch of hard candy. The Monsignor's shadow-fingers made a coaxing gesture: *Come on, kid; let's get the show on the road; cough it up.* This one time, Simone told me she heard that Monsignor "liked his liquor, too." But butter rum's not liquor, because if it was, how come *kids* can buy butter rum Life Savers?

I crossed myself and began. "Bless me, Father, for I have sinned. It has been two weeks since my last confession. These are my—"

A wheezy sigh interrupted me. "Speak up, boy. You're mumbling."

Well, of course I was. I was about to own up to a doozy that morning—a sin to which I did *not* want my peers to be privy, particularly Geraldine Balchunas, our class's biggest gossip who, as luck would have it, had stood at the front of the girls' line when

I'd slinked toward Monsignor's confessional seconds earlier. Behind Geraldine had stood my nemesis, Rosalie Twerski. Eavesdropping on other kids' confessions, our class had been assured, was sinful, and there was a strategy by which we could avoid this particular transgression. We were to close our eyes, cover our ears with our hands, and hum quietly to ourselves. This was small comfort, however, in my hour of need. Of the thirty-four of us, the number who actually used this technique was zero.

"It's been two weeks since my last confession," I began again. "These are my sins." I admitted that, having forgotten to do my sentence-diagramming homework one night, I had copied someone else's paper on the bus. That I had called my sister a retard twice. That swear words had come out of my mouth on six different occasions. "But not the really bad one, Monsignor. Just 'h' and 'd' and 's.'" I cleared my throat and mustered up my courage. "And ..."

Monsignor fished another Life Saver from his

roll and popped it in his mouth, crunching and waiting. "And *what?*" he finally asked.

"I . . . had impure thoughts."

"What was that last one? Speak up."

"I had these certain thoughts. . . . You know."

"No, I *don't* know, unless you tell me. What kind
of thoughts?"

"Impure ones. . . . About my cousin."

"Your *cousin?*"

"Yeah. My cousin Annette. She's famous." I could
practically see Geraldine and Rosalie out there, lean-
ing forward, their hands cupped behind their big
Dumbo ears.

"And did you act on these thoughts?" Monsignor
inquired.

Had I? Was French-kissing a poster as bad as
French-kissing a person? I told Monsignor I wasn't
sure.

"What do you mean, you're not sure? Either you
acted upon them or you didn't."

"I kissed her poster. . . . On the lips." I edited out the tongue part.

"Her poster? What do you—"

"The one of her at the beach. In her bathing suit, listening to her transistor. . . . But anyways, Monsignor, I'm sure glad you gave up cigarettes. My father used to smoke, too. Chesterfields. But then he—"

Monsignor cut me off and started telling me about how incest was a mortal sin, and how what I'd done made Jesus very, very, *very* sad. Had maybe even made Him weep, as He had the day He died on the cross for our sins. Then he gave me a *whole, entire* rosary to say for penance which, if I'd gotten Father Hanrahan, I probably would have had to say only a few "Our Father"s and "Hail Mary"s and maybe a "Glory Be."

"Now let's hear you make a good Act of Contrition," Monsignor said.

Unsure if I was apologizing to God or the Monsignor, I rattled from rote how "heartily sorry for having offended Thee" I was. But I was thinking, as

I recited the prayer, about how my impure thoughts were really more Pop's fault than mine. *He* was the one who'd led me into temptation by taping Annette's poster above the fryolator in the first place. And Chino's fault, too. I wouldn't have even known what French-kissing was if he hadn't told me. In a way, *they* should be saying whole rosaries for penance, not me.

Monsignor told me to imitate Jesus and gave me his blessing. Exiting the confessional, I tried to ignore Geraldine's and Rosalie's stares. "Take a picture. It lasts longer," I suggested as I passed by them on my way to the altar. I may have heard kissing sounds from one of them.

Later that day, while we were conjugating French verbs, the school secretary appeared at the back door of our classroom. *"Excusez-moi, mes élèves,"* Madame Frechette said. "Yes, Mrs. Tewksbury? May we help you?"

"Would you please excuse Felix Funicello for a few moments?" Mrs. T said. "There's someone down in the office who wishes to see him."

Approaching Mrs. Tewksbury on what seemed like my "perp walk," I felt the 66 eyes of my 33 classmates upon me. Out in the corridor, I asked Mrs. T who was waiting downstairs. "You'll see," she said. As I descended the staircases to the main floor, my mind raced with scenarios good and bad. Had a policeman come to deliver some grim news about my parents? Had my cousin Annette heard about me and come to St. Aloysius Gonzaga to make my acquaintance and, perhaps, to sign some autographs for my friends? Had a detective figured out that I was the one who'd awakened that bat and driven Sister Dymphna cuckoo? "They're waiting in Mother Filomina's office," Mrs. Tewksbury said. "You can go right in."

I heard Monsignor Muldoon's labored breathing as I approached the inner office. "Hello, Felix," Mother Filomina said. "Come in. Have a seat." She was behind her big desk, and the only available chair was the one opposite the Monsignor. I sat. He smiled, something I'd never seen him do before. He had little peg teeth, brownish from tar and nicotine, I figured. And little squiggly veins on his cheeks and in the yellowy whites of his eyes. And there were white hairs growing out of his nostrils. I was seated close enough to smell his blasts of butter rum breath, too.

"The Monsignor has brought you a gift," Mother Filomina said. "Wasn't that nice of him?" My head bobbed up and down, as if jerked by a puppeteer.

The Monsignor handed me a booklet, *Aloysius Gonzaga, Patron Saint of Male Youth*. There were veins on his hands, too, and big brown freckles. When he asked me if I knew much about the life of our school's namesake, I shook my head. I took a quick glimpse at the cover. It had a picture of Aloysius Gonzaga the Boy Saint, his hands clasped in prayer, his head surrounded by a big halo that kind of looked like an electric hula hoop.

"Have you anything to say to Monsignor?" Mother Filomina asked. I shook my head again. "No, Felix? Nothing at all?"

"Umm...How come you're giving me this?" When Mother cleared her throat, I finally caught her drift. "Oh. Thank you, I mean. Sorry."

The Monsignor said I was entirely welcome. "I think you'll find Aloysius's story inspirational, given what you and I talked about earlier today," he said. "He might be just the kind of boy whose example you would wish to emulate."

"Oh," I said. "Yeah?"

Mother Filomina frowned. "Yes, Monsignor."

"Yes, Monsignor," I repeated. On a *Dragnet* episode I'd seen once, Sergeant Joe Friday's arrest of a murderer had been thwarted by the confidentiality of the confessional, but apparently no such privilege was extended to kids and/or French-kissers. I didn't know how much Monsignor Magoo had told Mother Filomina about my confession, but I didn't really want to know, either. "Can I go now?" I asked her.

"*May* you go now?" Mother said. "Yes, you may."

Back in class, I stuck Monsignor's booklet in my social studies book, on top of the whoopee cushion

I'd forgotten to give back to Lonny. Geraldine Balchunas kept looking over at me, so I made cross-eyes at her. Rosalie got up to use the pencil sharpener, even though her pencil was sharp already. (Unlike Sister Dymphna, Madame Frechette let us get out of our seats and go over to the sharpener without asking.) "Pssst," Rosalie said, as she passed by me. "What did you have to go to the office for?"

I thought quickly about an answer that might really bug her. "Because I'm getting some big award," I said.

She went wide-eyed. "What for?"

"You writing a book?" I said. "Make that chapter a mystery."

"I'd rather write a monster story," she shot back. "About an ugly little dwarf named Dondi Funicello."

I told her her legs were so hairy she should comb them.

"Mademoiselle et monsieur!" Madame Frechette called to us. Red-faced, Rosalie rushed back to her seat. I flashed Madame my innocent Dondi smile.

At home after school that day, Ma was at one end of the kitchen table, doing the books for the business. I was seated at the opposite end, alternately tonguing the "surprise" out of the middle of a Hostess cupcake—why did they call it a surprise when it was always the exact same cream inside?— and drawing a picture of the PanAmerican jet that, the following Thursday, was gonna fly my mother to California. Simone was making supper—the same thing she always made when it was her turn: English muffin pizzas, salad, and lime Jell-O with Reddi-Wip for dessert.

"Are you ever going back to your regular hair?" I asked Ma.

She patted her beehive and smiled. "You like my old hairstyle better?"

"*Much* better," I assured her.

"Well, I guess I'll have to think about it then. Are you going to be okay while I'm gone?" I told her I didn't know yet because she hadn't left yet. She said that, after she came home from being on *her* TV show, she couldn't wait to see me on TV, too— *Ranger Andy*. Then she smiled and said that my father and sisters were going to take very, very good care of me until she got back. "Aren't you, Simone?" she asked.

"Yeah, sure," my sister said. "And don't listen to him about your hair, Ma. It looks real gear."

Ma smiled and, to me, said, "Is 'gear' good or bad?"

"Good," I said. "It's Beatles talk. Means 'groovy.'"

"Ah," she said. "Now maybe you'd better start your homework, huh?"

When I opened my social studies book to the chapter we were on, both Lonny's whoopee cushion and Monsignor's booklet revealed themselves. I looked again at the cover picture of Aloysius Gonzaga, then began thumbing through the pages. "A noble lad of Venice, he was so offended by the vulgar talk of the palazzo and the waterways that he would faint when he heard it," it said. It said, too, that Aloysius avoided females, even his own mother, and put chunks of wood in his bed at night to distract him from "temptations of the flesh." His hobbies—"mortifications," the book called them—were whipping himself, bathing lepers, and carrying away their slop pails. I wasn't positive, but I was pretty sure that slop pails meant buckets of shit. . . . *Merde! . . .* The booklet said Aloysius had died of some plague he caught while tending to the sick. This was who I was supposed to be like?

Well, I sure wasn't going to whip myself or bathe lepers, whatever they were. I could do the chunks of wood thing, though, I figured. So what I did was, before bed that night, I fished my can of Lincoln Logs out of the bottom of my toy chest and dumped them into bed with me. That lasted for about five minutes' worth of tossing and turning before my foot got an itch and I tried to scratch it with a Lincoln Log and it gave me a sliver. I sent the Lincoln Logs flying onto the floor. French-kissing Annette's poster might be the kind of sin that could get me cast into hell, but if heaven was going to be full of goody-goodies like Aloysius Gonzaga and Rosalie Twerski, then I figured I'd just go to H-E-double-toothpick instead. After all, Lonny was probably headed there. And Chino. And a bunch of our regulars down at the lunch counter.

It rained on Halloween, gently at first—a moist caress that made the glistening, streetlamp-lit fallen leaves slippery, but not the kind of rain that made your parents say you couldn't go trick-or-treating.

Lonny was a bum: rippy dungarees, a busted straw hat, and flannel shirt, and cheeks smeared with ash from his mother's ciggy butts. (He'd carried them over to my house in a Baggie.) A lot of people thought Lonny was Huckleberry Finn. I was Speedy Alka Seltzer, although so many people mistook me for a flying saucer that I started singing, "Plop, Plop.

Fizz Fizz. Oh, what a relief it is!" whenever home-owners opened their door. We were trick-or-treating for UNICEF, too.

Lonny said everyone in his neighborhood turned off their lights and sat in the dark because they were too cheap to buy kids candy, so he'd had to "borrow" my neighborhood. My mother told me that when she'd called Lonny's mother to see if he could sleep over, Mrs. Flood had said sure—we could keep him as long as we wanted, forever as far as she was con-cerned. She'd been joking, Ma said, but Ma hadn't thought it was very funny.

It felt pretty grown up trick-or-treating with just one of my friends; this was the first year Ma hadn't made my sisters take me, against their protests and mine. Lonny and I worked our way down Chestnut Street, then up Franklin and McKinley as far as War-ren Street, then right onto Broad Street, and back down Grove. "How can they not know you're a bum and I'm Speedy Alka Seltzer?" I sighed.

"Because people are idiots," Lonny said. "Get

used to it." Lightning illuminated him as he said it, then thunder cracked the sky. Seconds later, the sky let loose, soaking our costumes, our candy, and us. The cigarette soot on Lonny's cheeks dripped down his face and then washed away altogether and my sneakers were squishing with every step I took. The bottom of the First National bag I was using to trick-or-treat with gave way from the weight of my loot. "Let's go home," I said. Me and Lonny were transferring my candy from the sidewalk to his pillowcase when my father pulled up in our army green Studebaker. "You fellas need a lift?" he asked. We both got in the backseat, so it was kind of like Pop was our chauffeur. "Take us home, Salvatore," I said.

"Don't push it, wise guy," Pop said.

After we changed into our PJs, Lonny and I poured all our candy out onto my bed, divided it into piles, and traded. Ma told us we could each eat three things and then we had to stop. We could stay up until eleven o'clock, she said, and then it was lights off and go to sleep. "Do we *have* to go to church tomorrow?"

I whined. She said yes, we certainly did; it wasn't only Sunday but also All Saints Day—a holy day of obligation, which meant mandatory Mass on *two* counts, not just one.

"Well how come *he* never has to go?" I demanded, pointing to Pop.

"Because your father has a business to run," she countered. "And may I remind you, Mr. Knows Everything There Is to Know, that that business is what puts food on our table. Now maybe you should stop arguing with me and embarrassing yourself in front of your guest. What do you think?"

"Oh, I ain't embarrassed, Mrs. Funicello," Lonny assured her. "Our family fights all the time."

"Well, Lonny, that's very polite of you to say," Ma assured him. "But we're just having a discussion, not a fight."

"Oh," Lonny said.

Since Pop was in the room, I decided to negotiate. It worked, too. We got Ma to compromise: *five* pieces of candy each, an eleven thirty bedtime, and

Lonny and I didn't have to go to the 9:15 A.M. mass with my mother and sisters. Instead, free agents, we could go by ourselves to last mass at noon.

Of course, what Lonny and I had agreed to didn't mean that, once my bedroom door was closed, we had to stick to it. I ate nine pieces of candy and Lonny ate about *twice* that much. Hepped up on sugar, we had a tickling war and a pillow fight. Then we each opened our packs of Sugar Babies and NECCO Wafers and started whipping them at each other. When Lonny began pouring packets of Kool-Aid down his throat, I warned him that he was gonna get sick.

"No, I won't!" he insisted, and then, immediately after, began clutching his stomach and moaning. Then he ran to the corner of my room and started up-chucking. At least that was what I *thought* he was doing. "Are you okay?" I asked, approaching him cautiously. The two of us stood there looking at the pool of chunky brown puke on the floor. Then, to my horror, Lonny reached down, picked it up, and threw it at me. All's it was was *plastic* puke; he'd bought it off the Tricks & Jokes rack at Central Soda Shoppe so's he could fool me.

"Oh, that reminds me," I said. I went over to my desk, opened my social studies book, and took out his whoopee cushion.

"Hey, this is the one Dymphie took away from me," he said. "How'd you get it back?"

"That's for me to know and for you to find out," I said.

"No, really."

"I'm Robin Hood," I said. "I rob from the rich and give to the poor."

I thought Lonny would think that was funny, but he didn't. He got kind of mad, actually. His eyes got crazy and his nostrils opened and closed like a bull's in a bull fight. He shoved me up against the wall and held me there, his arm pressed against my chest. "What makes you think I'm *poor*?" he demanded.

"I *don't* think you are," I assured him (though I knew he was.) "All's I meant was that the teachers are like the bad guys and us kids are the good guys." I was on the verge of tears, either from the pressure against my chest or his sudden, unanticipated move against me. I wasn't sure which.

"Okay then," he said, and let go. "You gonna eat that Almond Joy or can I have it?" I handed it over.

At lights out, Lonny and me lay side by side in the dark. I was in my sleeping bag and he was borrowing my sister Frances's. At first, we were both quiet. Then, out of the blue, Lonny said, "Your father's old, isn't he?"

"Kind of," I said. "Older than my mother. She's 42 and he's 51. Why?"

"No reason. Did they have to get married?"

"Have to? Uh uh. They wanted to, I guess."

"Oh. Because my old man *had* to marry my old lady. Because my brother Denny was already in the oven, if you get my drift."

I didn't, but what he'd just said reminded me of that joke one of the sailors had told Chino down at the depot. "How is a woman like a stove?" I said. Lonny said he didn't know, and I said, "Because you gotta heat the oven up before you stick the meatloaf in." I still didn't get why that joke was funny, but Lonny laughed the exact same way Chino had.

Both of us were quiet some more, and I started wondering if Lonny'd already fallen asleep when he said, "You know something. You're lucky. My old man, when he used to live with us? If *he* knew I was out trick-or-treating in a thunderstorm, there's no way in hell he woulda come looking for me."

"How do *you* know?" I said. "Maybe he would have."

He laughed. "I can see you don't know my old man."

I couldn't think of anything to say that would make him feel better, so all's I said was, "Well, I'm getting kinda sleepy. G'night."

He reached over and poked me. "Night, shithead."

I poked him back and said what Frances always said whenever I called her a name. "I'm the rubber and you're the glue. Whatever you say bounces off me and sticks to you."

"Yeah, you're the rubber, all right," Lonny laughed. "For a teeny, tiny, little dickie." I wasn't sure if, when he said dickie, he meant a guy's you-know-what or one of those fake turtleneck things that kids wore under their shirts. But knowing Lonny, he probably meant the first thing.

"I know you are," I said. "But what am I? Gate's closed!" Which, when you say "gate's closed," it means the other person has to stop. So Lonny was the little dickie, not me.

The next morning after 9:15 mass, Ma had Simone drive her and Fran down to the lunch counter and then come back so she could make Lonny and me pancakes for breakfast. I was pushing it, I knew, when I asked Simone if we could have soda instead of milk and she said no. "What do you think, Felix? That you died and went to Heaven?"

Simone had set her hair and Scotch-taped her bangs because she had a modeling job that afternoon—some stupid fashion show that Ma was making me go to after we dropped Lonny back at his house. Lonny had a hoody older brother, Denny, but no sisters. "What are those things in your hair?" he asked Simone.

"Transmitters," I said. "She's a space alien. Her boyfriend is Robby the Robot." The last time Lonny had come over to my house, we'd watched the movie *Forbidden Planet* on Big 3 Theater.

Simone rolled her eyes. "They're Spoolies," she said.

Lonny kept looking over at her while she was making our pancakes. Looking at her funny, I mean—mouth-breathing and swallowing like he was thirsty. Every time he'd swallow, his Adam's apple would go up and down. What the heck was the matter with *him*, I wondered.

And then in the middle of eating our pancakes, Lonny said to Simone, "Aren't you having any?" She said she was going to, but that first she had to put away all the stuff.

"I'll help you," Lonny said. He got up. Grabbed the milk and eggs and put them back in the fridge. I didn't get why he was acting so weird. "Come on, Simone," he said, "Sit down and eat before these delicious pancakes get cold."

She smiled and nodded. Placed her plate on the table. But when she sat down, there was this fart that was so loud it practically broke the sound barrier!

Simone jumped up, mortified, and looked down at her chair.

"Gotcha!" Lonny guffawed.

She picked up his whoopee cushion and started whacking him with it: once, twice, three times, four. Then, giggling, she put her hands around his neck and pretended she was choking him. It *was* pretty funny, and I was laughing, too, kind of—and then, all of a sudden, I wasn't. Because I could see Lonny's you-know-what poking up from inside his pajama bottoms. And I guess Simone must have seen it, too, because she said, "Oh!" and ran out of the kitchen. And that was the last either of us saw of her that morning.

Later, walking over to St. Aloysius for noon mass, Lonny said, "You know what we should do? Ditch church and go to the movies instead." I reminded him that it was not just Sunday but also All Saints Day—the Catholic church's equivalent of a baseball double-header. "Yeah?" he said. "So what?"

"So what are we going to buy our tickets with? Our *looks*?" Pop used that line whenever my sisters and me argued that we should buy a color TV like the Shaefers next door: and what do you kids suggest we should use for a down payment? Our looks?

"How about we use *this*?" Lonny said. He reached into his coat pocket, took out his UNICEF carton, and shook it like a castanet.

"We can't!" I said, shocked that he could even suggest such a thing. "That's stealing from kids who are *starving*." Lonny may very well have been the dumbest kid in our class, grade book-wise, but his response was brilliant.

"Oh, okay, Rosalie. I guess you're right."

"Rosalie? I ain't her! How come I'm her?"

"Oh, that's right. You're Felix. I always get you goody-two-shoes girls mixed up."

Ma had always vetoed my going to scary movies on the pretext that they might give me nightmares, but here's what Lonny and I saw that day: this really, *really* scary movie called *Hush . . . Hush, Sweet Charlotte*. It was about this guy who, long ago, had gotten his head chopped off with a meat cleaver, and everyone thought this weird woman named Charlotte did it. Except she hadn't. I recognized the lady who played Charlotte; she was the same lady who'd played Apple Annie in another movie that Frances, Simone, and I had seen the Christmas before called *Pocketful of Miracles*. *Pocketful of Miracles* had been in color, but *Hush . . . Hush, Sweet Charlotte* was in black and white, which somehow made it even scarier. There was this piano that played all by itself and a bunch of other creepy stuff. When that guy got murdered with the meat cleaver at the beginning of the movie, I closed my eyes, but Lonny caught me and made fun of me and said I was Mr. Chicken, *cluck, cluck, cluck*. So later, when this other guy got *his* head chopped off and the head went bouncing down the stairs, I had to force myself to keep looking, even though I didn't want to. And after? When we were walking out of the show? Lonny said he thought *Hush . . . Hush, Sweet Charlotte* stunk and wasn't scary. What did *I* think?

"Huh? . . . Oh, yeah. It stunk worse than a skunk. You call *that* scary? Gimme a break. We should've asked for our money back."

What I'd really been thinking was that Ma had been right—I *was* going to probably get nightmares, which, whenever I got them, I'd get up and go to her and Pop's bedroom and tap her on the shoulder and go, "Ma?" and she'd get out of bed and stumble back down to my room and sit in my chair until I got back to sleep. Except what was I supposed to do if I got a nightmare about that guy's head bouncing down the stairs while she was all the way across the country in California? And plus, was I now going to have to let Monsignor Muldoon know that, not only had I French-kissed my cousin's poster, but also that I'd skipped church on a Sunday *and* a holy day so that I could go to the movies instead, and that we'd bought our tickets with UNICEF money that was supposed to be for poor kids who could drink milk for a whole month for like two pennies or something? . . . Except it was *Lonny's* UNICEF money, not mine, I reminded myself. My own UNICEF carton, heavy with dimes, quarters, nickels, and half dollars would be turned in dutifully on Monday morning. Where was the sinning in that?

Monday was always Current Events day in Madame Frechette's class, which meant that our weekend homework included looking through magazines and newspapers and cutting out articles that might get thumb-tacked to the side bulletin board titled "Our Town, Our Nation, & Our World." On Mondays, after lunchtime recess, we were called, one by one, to stand, walk to the front of the room, and summarize our articles. That Monday, November 2, 1964, several of my classmates reported on stuff about the next day's Presidential election. Ronald Kubiak told us that Dr. Martin Luther King had broken his rule of not endorsing either candidate and was now urging colored people—*black* people! I keep forgetting—to vote for LBJ, not Goldwater. Oscar Landry quoted President Johnson himself: "We are not going to send American boys nine or ten thousand miles away from home to do what Asian boys ought to be doing for themselves." Geraldine Balchunas predicted that, if Johnson got reelected, it was entirely possible that one of his daughters, Lynda Bird or Lucy Baines, would have a White House wedding.

Jackie Burnham informed us that Great Britain had elected its youngest prime minister ever, Harold somebody, and Edgy Chang reported that the Boston police had rounded up a suspect in the Boston Strangler murders. (Edgy's real name is Doris, but everyone calls her Edgy on account of when her mother was pregnant with her, she was always real nervous.) When Edgy spoke in detail about the Strangler's gruesome methods, Madame cut her off with a *"Merci, mademoiselle."* She called on Lonny Flood.

Lonny stood, sauntered to the front of the room, and, with a yawn, informed us that the previous Saturday had been Halloween. We waited.

"And what of that?" Madame finally said.

Lonny shrugged. "That's it. That it was Halloween. . . . And, oh yeah, it rained. On Halloween. Which was Saturday." He returned to his desk and sat.

Rosalie Turdski raised her hand in protest. "That's not really a current event," she said. "It's just something that was on the calendar."

In defense of Lonny, I raised *my* hand. "It wasn't on the calendar that it rained. That was the current events part of it: that it rained."

Madame looked unconvinced, and I was pretty

sure that the mark she recorded in her grade book for Lonny was yet another check minus. "Rosalie," she said. "Would you like to go next?" And when she did, I was furious! Because rat-fink Rosalie had clipped the exact same item from the paper that I had—the article about how a local woman, Mrs. Marie Funicello, my *mother*, not *hers*, would later that week compete for the grand prize in the Pillsbury Bake-Off. "And I just want to say that I have fingers and toes crossed, and that I'm praying every single night that Mrs. Funicello . . . that Mrs. Funicello . . ."

Rosalie stopped abruptly, upstaged and rendered speechless. At the back door of our classroom stood Mother Filomina with a broad-faced man in a long black coat and a wooly black hat and a broad-faced look-alike girl who was grinning from ear to ear. Besides her plaid St. Aloysius jumper, she was wearing an oversized crushed velvet Carnaby Street–style cap, bubble gum pink, and Cheeto-colored knee socks, and black galoshes with metal clips. Shockingly, she was also wearing blue eye shadow. (Makeup was strictly forbidden by St. Aloysius Gonzaga's Code of Conduct. The only exception, I knew from my sisters, was for eighth grade girls at the final graduation dance, when they could wear lipstick, plus nylons.) Zhenya's hair was plaited in long, greasy, brown braids. She had pierced ears. She had "bazoom-booms."

"Khello, clissmates!" she proclaimed. "I em Zhenya Kabakova, and I em veddy, veddy kheppy to mek you acqueentinks! Khello, new frinds! Khello! Khello!"

Rosalie's mouth dropped open like a glove compartment door with a busted latch. November, I figured, had just gotten more interesting.

4

Zhenya

My classmates and I were standoffish with Evgeniya "Zhenya" Kabakova at first. It probably didn't help that she arrived at school each morning arm-in-arm with either her mother, her father, or both. And that half the time, as they entered the schoolyard, they were singing what I guessed were Russian songs. Zhenya's mother was a short, squat woman with a limp and a missing tooth. "Mrs. Khrushchev," we nicknamed her. Zhenya's father, with his wooly black hat, long coat, and droopy mustache, reminded me of those guards at the Wicked Witch's castle in *The Wizard of Oz*. Mr. Kabakov had a strange little ritual that he performed each time he brought his daughter to school. First he'd bend and kiss Zhenya on the forehead. Then, as she turned away from him, he would lift his foot and give her a playful little kick in the rear end. After a while, the gesture became pretty predictable, but Zhenya never failed to giggle with astonished delight whenever her father booted her.

Zhenya was nice enough—friendly and cheerful, *exuberant*, even. (In vocabulary, we'd had to use the word "exuberant" in a sentence, and I'd written, "Our new classmate is very <u>exuberant</u>.) But each morning she smelled kind of like mayonnaise and, after lunch, definitely like fish. (Madame had assigned her to a desk one row over, so she was my right-side neighbor.) We watched her like hawks, boys *and* girls, in those first days. In the cafeteria at lunchtime, she didn't take hot lunch; she brought her own. Surrounded by empty chairs, Zhenya would remove from a brown paper bag (a *grocery* bag, not a lunch bag) some weird-looking crackers and a square-shaped tin of herring. She'd pull the key from the bottom of the can and open it, then scoop out chunks of the oily fish with her crackers and eat contentedly, unaware of, or un-bothered by, the fact that she was being shunned. Whenever she looked over at us, smiling and waving, we'd quickly look away and then, a few seconds later, resume our staring.

One day during class discussion—I forgot how it came up—Zhenya revealed that she was thirteen years old, not ten like the rest of us, except for Lonny who, because he'd stayed back twice, was twelve and a half. She also divulged that the reason she smelled like mayonnaise was because her mother conditioned her hair with it, as did the mothers of "minny, minny geuhls in Soviet Union." We all looked at each other, shocked, and Madame Frechette said something in *québecois* that, she explained, meant, "To each his own taste." Speaking of which, Ma had left the day before to compete in the Pillsbury Bake-Off.

Writing absentee excuses to the powers-that-be at St. Aloysius Gonzaga was usually my mother's domain, and so a look of panic crossed Pop's face that morning when I told him he'd have to write the note to get me sprung early. A maestro of the lunch counter, Pop was not exactly zippity-doo-da when it came to writing. (Like Chino, he was a high school dropout. But *unlike* Chino, who'd quit school because he suspected the lunch ladies were serving their students Gravy Train, Pop, the eldest of six kids, had had to quit to help his widowed mother support her family.)

Dear Whoever Is Suppose to get this Note,
    Please excuse Felix Funicello at 1 o'clock today so he can walk downtown to the Bus Station, we're having a little shindig down at our Lunch Counter and he will get to

see his mother on TV. Which will be very educational. Your
all invited, anyone who wants to come down there.

Your's Truly,

Salvatore P. Funicello

Pop had been fixing me breakfast when I hit him up for that note, and he concentrated so hard while composing it that he burned the bottoms of my pancakes. When I complained about them, he threw the spatula into the sink real hard and told me to quit my goddamned belly-aching. "Just eat from the top down and leave the rest!" It was weird, and a little scary, to witness my father blowing his top like that; he was usually the most even-tempered of men. Reading over his note as I attempted to surgically remove the burnt parts of my pancakes, I was pretty sure that Mother Filomina would be horrified by my father's fragments and run-on sentences, not to mention his spelling, capitalization, and punctuation mistakes. Still, I decided not to suggest that he do it over. For one thing, I didn't want to make him even madder.

And for another, I figured Mother Fil might marvel at the giant leap forward I represented, grammar- and usage-wise. Given Pop's note, how could she miss that evolutionary miracle?

But poor Pop. He was overwhelmed by Ma's five-day absence and real nervous about that afternoon's "shindig." He was planning to lug our nineteen-inch black-and-white TV down to the depot, jury-rig a temporary antenna in hopes of pulling in the Bake-Off finals, and serve the assembled free coffee and pie à la mode. He'd ordered nine pies from the Mama Mia Bakery, five apple and four blueberry. "I just hope to hell that'll be enough," I overheard him telling Simone. Her and Frances were getting out of school early, too.

Everybody at my school that day kept telling me they thought Ma was going to win. And hey, hadn't they all been right, two days earlier, about the President? In St. Aloysius's mock election, LBJ had beaten AuH$_2$0 in every single grade. (And then beaten him for real, too—a "landslide" the newspaper had called it.) During morning P.A. announcements, Sister Fabian, the vice-principal, said that everyone at St. Aloysius Gonzaga was hoping my mother won. After lunch, our whole class said a prayer for her. And when it was time for me to get excused, Madame Frechette hugged me—as usual, her lily-of-the-valley perfume gave me a sneezing attack—and said she wished my mother *bonne chance*, heh heh heh. Out in the corridor, even our janitor, Mr. Dombrowski, stopped mopping and gave me the V-for-victory sign. Jeezum, I thought as I trudged down to the bus station: Ma was practically as famous as Annette.

Counting bus travelers and regular customers, 63 people gathered at the lunch counter to watch that afternoon's special edition of *Art Linkletter's House Party*, plus have their free pie and coffee. Pop had set up our TV at the end of the counter, and Joey Cigar from Joey's Newsstand & Smoke Shoppe on the other side of the depot had helped him hook up this special Sputnik-looking antenna on top. The picture was snowy, but you could still see everything pretty good, especially when Joey had his brother-in-law, Frankie, hold on to the end of the long wire that trailed down from the Sputnik thing. "We finally found something that Frankie's good for," I overheard Joey telling Chino. "Pulling in television signal."

We fed everybody first. Pop cut the pies, Frances scooped the ice cream, and me and Simone passed people their plates. Chino was in charge of the coffees. "Cowboy" Zupnik came with this lady, Noreen, and I was like, whoa, the Cowboy's got a *wife*? But Noreen was his sister. She said we should start selling Shepherd's Pie Italiano at the lunch counter, and everybody said, yeah, yeah, that was a great idea. Cindy Creamcheese said she'd even skip eating her pepperoni omelet to try a piece, and Chino said, maybe she'd better not, because if she actually ordered something different than her usual, it might give him and Sal a heart attack. (He was only kidding.) Cindy Creamcheese brought her son Christopher with her, which, I didn't even know she *had* a kid. He was about my age, and real fat like his mother, and I thought, wow, that sure is a weird name: Christopher Creamcheese. He finished his free pie à la mode in about two seconds, licked his plate, and asked me if he could have seconds. I asked Pop and he said no, just one to a customer. Christopher was kind of a pest because he kept following me around wherever I went, like he was my shadow or something. Oh, and Reverend Peavey? He was there. He came with this sailor he was doing missionary work on, except they had to leave before the Bake-Off came on, because they had to go pray or something. And Mush Moriarty came, too, but when Pop asked him did he want any pie, he said no, but he'd take a Four Roses, neat, and Pop pointed at the door and he left.

Simone moved through the crowd, handing out the pie à la modes and bragging to everybody about how, the day after she flew to California, Ma went to visit Annette's parents at their *house* on account of Pop was Annette's father's *cousin*, and he and Ma had gone to Annette's parents' *wedding*, and when Simone was a baby, she'd been in the same *playpen* with

Annette—there was even a *picture* of it. And how, even though Ma hadn't exactly seen Annette when she went over to her parents' house—which was real beautiful, by the way—she *had* seen the room where they kept all of Annette's souvenirs and stuff, including this *huge* framed color picture of her with Walt Disney in front of Cinderella's castle at Disneyland that said, on the bottom, *To America's Sweetheart and her Wonderful Family! With my very fondest wishes, "Uncle" Walt.*

Simone was in the middle of telling the eight billionth person about Ma's going to Annette's parents' house when Frances, who could whistle the loudest out of anyone in our whole family, stuck two fingers in her mouth, let go a real loud one, and shouted, "Hey! Shush up, everybody! It's coming on!" Everyone crowded in closer to the TV, all's except Frankie, who grabbed onto the end of the wire and made the picture stop snowing. It was kinda cool, I thought, the way he was like this human antenna. "S'cuse me, s'cuse me," I kept saying until I'd squeezed my way up to the front.

First, Art Linkletter said the Pillsbury Bake-Off was like the kitchen Olympics, except instead of athletes competing, the contestants were "the best bakers all across the U.S. of A." Then he explained the categories and contest rules and reminded the audience that nothin' said lovin' like somethin' from the oven, and that Pillsbury said it best. Then the camera went from him to this big, giant room at the Beverly Hills Hilton Hotel where all these stoves—a hundred of them, one for both winners from each state—had been hooked up so's that the ninety-eight women and two men who were trying for the $25,000 grand prize could cook their recipes. And every single state winner had the exact same Pillsbury Bake-Off apron on, even those two men.

"And now, let's check in with my good friend, the handsome star of the silver screen and the genial host of *General Electric Theater*," Art Linkletter said. "And by the way, here's a scoop for you, folks. This coming season, he'll replace The Old Ranger as your narrator on *20 Mule Team Borax's Death Valley Days*. That's right, ladies and gents. You know who I mean: none other than Mr. Ronald Reagan. Take it away, Ronnie!"

"Heh heh heh," Ronald Reagan said, kind of like Madame Frechette. At first, I closed my eyes and looked away because I thought it was the same guy whose chopped-off head had bounced down the stairs in *Hush . . . Hush, Sweet Charlotte*. But then I squinted and saw that it was a different guy. (Later on, I checked the movie ads in the newspaper, and it said the chopped-off-head guy was this other guy named Joseph Cotten.) Ronald Reagan's job was to walk around the big room—the *ball*room, he called it— with a microphone that had this long, long cord and talk to the state winners. Which, you could tell what states they were from by these cardboard flags stick- ing up on poles behind their General Electric stoves. A lady from Nebraska said she was making a dessert called "Nebraska Baked Alaska." And another lady gave Ronald Reagan a taste of this appetizer she in- vented called "Zelda's Zesty Welsh Rabbit," and I went to Frances, who was standing next to me, I went,

"Yuck! You wouldn't catch me eating that. Rabbits are in the *rodent* family."

And Fran said, "It's *rare*bit, not rabbit, you idiot." And I said she was the idiot, not me, and she said, "I'm the rubber and you're the glue. Anything you say bounces off me and sticks to you."

"Oh, yeah? Well, you're—"

"Keep quiet and listen, you two!" Pop said, slapping the backs of both our heads on account of Ronald Reagan had just said, "Now let's see what's cookin' with the gals from the Nutmeg State." And everyone at the lunch counter started whooping and hollering and squeezing in closer.

The camera zoomed in on Mrs. Parzych, the other Connecticut winner. She told Ronald Reagan how she'd invented "Creamy Dreamy Sweetheart Torte" out of leftover cake that she'd made from a Pillsbury cake mix, plus cream cheese and whipping cream that had gone bad in her refrigerator but that she didn't want to just throw out because she's thrifty. And Ronald Reagan went "Sweetheart torte, eh? And who's *your* sweeheart?" and she said it was her husband, Stanley. Here's what I didn't get: nobody was at the stove next to Mrs. Parzych's—which was Ma's, I figured—but you could hear her oven timer going off like nyyyyyyyyyyyyyyyeeeeeeeee-aaaaaaaaaaa.

I pulled on Frances's sleeve. "Where's Ma?" I said. Me and Ronald Reagan must have had ESP or something, because before Fran could even answer me, he goes to Mrs. Parzych, "Now what's become of your Connecticut cohort?" Mrs. Parzych fidgeted with her fingers and looked away from Ronald Reagan and said, well, that Ma was coming right back but that she'd had to make a quick visit to the toilet.

"Jesus Christ and Jiminy Cricket!" Pop shouted in front of everybody. "Marie's got the trots! Same as she always does when she's a nervous wreck!" Pop must have been pretty nervous, too, I figured. Why else would he be making an announcement to sixty-something people about Ma having diarrhea?

In support of her "Connecticut cohort," Mrs.

Parzych silenced the stove timer, pulled on a pair of plaid mitts, and took Ma's dish out of the oven. It was all smoky, and the Pillsbury crescent rolls that formed the top crust looked kinda burnt. Everybody at the lunch counter got real quiet, except for someone way in the back that said, "Uh oh."

And then? On TV? There was Ma, running in from the right. Her beehive was kinda wobbling from side to side, and there was this weird white thing flying behind her that reminded me of the surrender flag they waved sometimes in cowboy movies. When Ronald Reagan seen Ma coming at him, he looked kinda scared, and he said, "So let's see what's cookin' down in Louisiana! Mimi's Mumbo Jumbo Gumbo! Now *that* sounds pretty darn delicious, doesn't it?" And instead of walking toward the Louisiana lady's stove, he sort of broke into a run.

As it turned out, that white thing flying behind Ma *was* sort of like a flag of surrender. After she'd finished her diarrhea, she'd somehow gotten toilet paper stuck in her apron strings and the elastic waistband of her skort. I was pretty sure, even *before* they announced that "Sandra's E-Z Tuna Stroganoff with Pillsbury Biscuits" was the winner in Ma's category and that "Coco-Nutty Blond Brownie Bars" was getting the $25,000 grand prize, that that 1965 Buick Riviera with the hideaway headlights wasn't going to end up parked in our driveway. "Booooooo!" I said when Art Linkletter shook hands with the winners. Simone slugged me one and told me to stop being a poor sport. Then she said to go ask my teachers if they wanted any pie and coffee. "What do you mean, my teachers?" I said.

I looked back to where my sister was pointing, and there were Sister Fabian, Sister Lucinda, and Mother Filomina. Nuns from my school at our lunch counter? It was like some kind of psycho dream! I didn't want to go over to them, but Simone and Pop both made me.

Sister Lucinda wanted pie but no ice cream— apple, which was good because there was no more blueberry. Mother Filomina said she'd take a little bit of ice cream but no pie. Sister Fabian said no thanks, she didn't want anything. Christopher Cream-cheese, who was still shadowing me, said, "Can I have hers then?" So I told him okay, but this time he couldn't lick his plate because it was bad manners. And he said if it was gonna be his pie, then yes he could so lick the plate, and I said, "Okay, fine, no pie then," and he said all right, all right, he wouldn't. And after I gave it to him, he said, "You know what? You're weird" and I said, "So ain't you." And he stuck his tongue out at me and there was ice cream and pie crust all over it. But at least he stopped fol-lowing me around.

"Well, Felix, you must be very proud of your mother," Sister Fabian said. I wasn't sure when she and the others had arrived, but I figured it had to have been after Ma'd come out of the bathroom, trailing toilet paper and scaring Ronald Reagan.

"Yeah," I said. "I mean, yes, Sister. . . . Sisters. And Mother."

"Why, you're entirely welcome, Felix," Mother

Filomina said. "And I hope you know how proud *we* are of *you*."

"Huh?" I said. I didn't know what I'd done that they should be proud of me for, but still, I thought, it was too bad Rosalie wasn't there because it probably would've killed her to hear Sister say it to me, not her.

In a long distance call from her hotel room that night—you could hear both sides of Ma's and Pop's conversation because they were both using these real loud long-distance voices—Ma verified that her nerves had given her the runs just before the broadcast began. Her fellow contestants had been very nice about her having burned her Shepherd's Pie Italiano, she said. But still, she'd been mortified—about that and about the toilet paper. She asked Pop if you could see it on TV and he lied and said, no, no, the only thing you could see was how beautiful she looked—that in his opinion, she was the most beautiful woman in that whole big room. Ma said she couldn't wait to come home. "Well, Tootsy Cake, we can't wait for you to *get* home either," Pop assured her. "I haven't had a decent night's sleep since you left." He looked at me when he said the last part, and I couldn't really blame him.

Because, as I had feared while I was watching *Hush . . . Hush, Sweet Charlotte* with Lonny that day, Joseph Cotten's stupid bouncing head had haunted me nightly in Ma's absence. Some nights it wouldn't let me get to sleep, and some nights it woke me up. Either way, I'd wait a while, listening to the chiming of our downstairs clock every fifteen minutes, and then finally have to get out of bed, go down the hall to my parents' room, and tap my father on the shoulder. "Pop?" I'd whisper. Wait. "Pop? Yoo hoo? . . . HEY, POP!" By then, I wasn't so much tapping his shoulder as pounding on it.

"Mffph? Wha . . . ?"

"I'm thinking about it again."

"Thinking about . . . ?"

"That head."

He squashed his pillow over his own head. "Jesus Christ, Felix, how many times I gotta tell you that it's just your imagination? Go back to sleep."

"I can't. Unless—"

"Look, I've sat up with you for three nights now. I need my sleep, Felix. You're turning me into a zombie."

I'd seen a zombie movie on *Channel 8 Shock Theater* a while back and they scared me, too. "Please, Poppa. *Pleeease.*"

Pop came up with a new solution. For that night and the next—the last two nights of Ma's absence—he let me sleep in my sleeping bag on the floor in his and Ma's bedroom. And when Frances snuck in the second night and rolled that cantaloupe at me, chanting, "Ooooo, Felix, it's the head! Oooooo," and I started screaming? It woke Pop up *again*, and he got so mad at Fran that he chased her all around the house, and when he caught her, he kicked her in the fanny, kind of like Zhenya's father did to Zhenya in the schoolyard, except not kidding around like Mr.

Kabakov. Not hard, though, either. And the next day? For her punishment? Frances had to come right home after school instead of going to field hockey practice and wash all the downstairs windows in our house, inside and out, plus the storm windows, too, even though they weren't even that dirty, except for the two where I stuck my fingers in the peanut butter jar and wrote on the glass *FF was here* and *Hi Frances Ha Ha.*

After Ma arrived home from California, she kept getting all these consolation prizes in the mail: cases of Nestlé cocoa and quilted Kaiser aluminum foil, a big basket of jams from Knott's Berry Farm, a spice rack, a G.E. electric mixer, and this other new G.E. thing, an electric knife. Oh, and along with all her consolation prizes, Ma also got a copy of the judges' comments about her Shepherd's Pie Italiano. (The judges had judged all the food the day before the TV show, so they didn't judge Ma's burnt Shepherd's Pie Italiano; they judged the one she made the day before.) One judge said Ma's recipe was "quite good, quite inventive" and another judge called it "scrumptious." The third judge was snotty, though. Ma figured it was probably the stuck-up lady judge who'd worn a pillbox hat and a jacket with a mink collar and had acted all full of herself. She'd written, "To my mind, the ground lamb & Niblets mixture combined with tomato sauce does not make for a happy marriage."

Simone was setting her hair with juice-can rollers while Ma read her the snotty judge's comment. "Oh, I know *that* type," she said. Then she mimicked her. "The marriage of ground lamb and *tomahto* sauce should get a divorce."

For a while, it became a family joke. "Would you care for orange juice or *tomahto* juice?" Or at Sunday dinner, "This marriage of *tomahto* sauce and Marie's macaroni and meatballs is simply exquisite, is it not?"

"Indeed it is, Mrs. La Di Da. Now be a *dahling* and *pahss* me the *cahviar.*"

✳　✳　✳

Zhenya Kabakova won over Madame Frechette first, perhaps because of what they had in common: both were weird; both were foreigners; both were inexplicably cheerful despite having been assigned second-class status by their respective majorities—in Zhenya's case, her "clissmates," and in Madame's case, the Sisters of Charity. (Carrying a note to the office one afternoon for Madame, I'd passed Sister Cecelia and Sister Godberta kibitzing in the hallway and overheard one of them whisper something not very charitable about "the Canadian in her tight sweaters.")

Lonny Flood was the next to fall to Zhenya's curious charms, possibly because they were close to the same age, or because Zhenya had had a considerable head-start over her female peers with regard to bazoom-boom development, or both. In class, Zhenya was sweet, but out on the playground, she was salty—as salty as Lonny, even. No, saltier. Lonny took it upon himself to teach her dirty American slang and she was all-aboard for his tutorial.

"Say this," he'd say. "Go shit in your hat."

"Go sheet een you het," Zhenya would repeat. But the mentoring went both ways. "H'okay, Lunny, now you say thees: *Ya zhópay chuvstuyu, chto menya sevodnya vyzovyet directora shkoly.*"

Lonny did his best to repeat what he'd just heard. "What'd I say? What'd I say?" he demanded.

"You sed yode ess says you gunna hef to go to principal's offees today!"

Lonny turned to me. "What's yode ess?" he asked. In response, I kicked him in his. "Oh! My ass!" he said, laughing. Then, to Zhenya, he said. "Come on! Give me another one!"

"H'okay. Ripit ifter me, Lunny. *Ón igráyet s Dúnkăy Kulakóvăy.*"

Lonny imitated his tutor and asked again what dirty thing he'd just spoken. In her broken English, Zhenya told him he'd said he was playing with Dick McFist. Lonny doubled over with laughter, as did Zhenya. "I don't get it," I said. "Who's Dick McFist?"

"She just taught me how to say, like, 'He's play-ing with Mrs. Palm and her five daughters,'" Lonny explained—or tried to.

I shrugged "I *still* don't get—" Lonny dropped his hand down there and made a gesture as if he were doing what Chino Molinaro referred to as "diddling yourself." "Oh," I said. "Okay. Now I get it."

At which point, Zhenya shrieked in comic hor-ror. "Lunny, ha ha, you a *pizdăstradátil!*" she declared. I followed her pointing finger to his you-know-what, which was poking out the same way it had that morning when Simone had sat on Lonny's whoopie cushion and then pretended to choke him. I looked away and asked Zhenya what a *pizda*-whatever-it-was was. "How you say it? A hoorny boy. A pooh, pooh boy who has prublem like Meek Jagguh in Rulling Stuns: he kent git no satisfacting, he kent git no geuhl reacting."

Embarrassed by Zhenya's pointing and her re-marks, Lonny turned his back to us and ran doubled-over to the edge of the school yard. With his fingers gripping the chain-link fence, he looked out at the passing cars. And when the bell rang, he was the last to reenter the building. "Lunny, you noty, noty boy!" Zhenya called over her shoulder with a laugh as she climbed the stairs. "Where go'd thet feeshing pole een-side you paints?" Yeah, she was definitely the saltier one.

If Zhenya's sexual awareness was what had piqued Lonny's interest, it was her athletic prowess that won over the rest of us fifth grade boys. She could fire a dodge ball with such force and precision that the Kubiak twins' reign as "ends" was over. Uninterested in jumping rope like the other girls, and uninvited by them to do so, she played baseball with us boys in-stead. Bezbull, she pronounced it. Zhenya could field, she could hit, and, man oh man, could she pitch. "I peecher today, h'okay, fellas?" she'd ask. It got so, when we chose up, whichever captain got "first picks" picked Zhenya. "I good bezbull player, eh, Fillix?" she asked me. "Mebbey I gooder player then Meeky Moose, ya?"

"Mickey Mouse, you mean?"

"Ya, ya. Meeky *Mouse*. He good bezbull player, ya?"

"I guess so," I said, shrugging. "For a cartoon."

"Nyet, Fillix. He no cartun. He play for H'Yinkees in Bronx, Noo H'Yoke."

"Oh, okay," I said. "You mean Mickey *Mantle*."

She laughed at her error. "Oh! H'okay, Fillix! I mek meestake. Meeky *Mantle* eez bezbull player. Mickey *Moose* eez cartun."

One day Zhenya brought to school, inside a blue cloth bag, her father's "shout poot." I was happy for Lonny, who, at recess that day, threw the shot put the farthest of anyone. Franz Duzio and Ernie Overturf came in second and third, respectively. But Zhenya's throw landed further than any of the other boys in class, myself included. At the end of recess, Sister Godberta, who had playground duty that day, confiscated Zhenya's father's shot put and told Zhenya she could have it back at the end of the day but should not bring it back to school again. And sure enough, at closing announcements, Mother Filomina came on the P.A. to inform all St. Aloysius Gonzaga students that shot-putting had been added to the list of forbidden activities, along with wearing makeup, writing hurtful things about others in opinion books, getting a Beatles haircut, and girls pulling the "fruit loops" off the backs of the boys' blue uniform shirts. From my desk to the left of her, I heard Zhenya mumble, "No shout poot? Thet eez boolshit. Thees boolshit skool."

Rosalie Twerski led the girls' campaign against Zhenya. She was critical of her boyish play, her indestructible cheerfulness, her mangling of grammar and pronunciation, and her pierced ears. (Unlike makeup and shot-putting, pierced ears were allowable by the rules of the St. Aloysius Gonzaga Code of Conduct, possibly because of their connection to saintly self-mutilation.) One morning, Rosalie came to school armed with a new poster. It was titled *What You Should Know About Communism—AND WHY!!!!!* Beneath the numbered, hand-lettered charges Rosalie had made against the evil Soviets, she'd drawn and colored a picture of the Kremlin and, in front of that, had glued magazine pictures of the new Russian leaders, Aleksei Kosygin and bushy-eyebrowed Leonid Brezhnev. Cartoon bubbles hovered over each. "We will conquer the world!" Kosygin declared. Brezhnev warned, "We will atom-bomb the U.S.A. and take over your country and turn it COMMUNIST!!" It had yet to be established whether or not our newest "clissmate" and her family were members of the Communist party, but given Zhenya's playground prowess, it had come to seem irrelevant to us boys. It was apparently irrelevant to Madame as well, because when she took Rosalie's poster from her, she told her she would give her extra credit for it and then exiled it to the closet.

"Aren't you going to hang it up?" Rosalie wanted to know.

"At some later date, *peut-être*," Madame told her.

"Well, I hope so. Because I worked really, really, *really* hard on it."

"*Oui, mademoiselle.* So noted. Now please take your seat."

Rosalie heaved a disgusted sigh and walked to her desk, rolling her eyes and mumbling about the number of hours she'd spent on her stupid poster.

On the Monday morning before Thanksgiving vacation, during Current Events, kids' reports included the news that President Kennedy's perpetual flame had drawn thousands of people to his grave at Arlington National Cemetery on the first anniversary of him getting assassinated. And that Mariner 4 had been launched successfully toward Mars. And that South Vietnam had destroyed a bunch of secret underground Viet Cong tunnels. Kitty Callahan, who was our class's biggest Beatlemaniac, said that, according to something called *Variety*, the Beatles were the Entertainers of the Year on account of their 45s had hit #1 for seventeen different weeks and *A Hard Day's Night* was the second most popular movie of the year after *Mary Poppins*.

During the part where you got to ask the speaker

a question about their Current Event, Marion Pemberton raised his hand and Kitty nodded. "Are you sure it's the Beatles and not the Four Tops or the Supremes?"

"Uh uh," Kitty said, shaking her head. "It's definitely the Beatles."

"Oh, man," Marion exclaimed. And three or four of us boys said it along with him. "Wait'll the NAACP hears about *this!*"

Geraldine Balchunas was the last Current Events person. Her report was about some experiment up in Hartford called "subscription television" where you had to pay for TV instead of getting it for free. During the part where you got to ask the speaker a question about their Current Event, I raised my hand. Geraldine pulled her mouth to the side of her face, none too pleased. "Felix?"

"That would be like going to a store and *buying* water instead of just getting it out of the sink," I said.

"Yeah? So?"

"So why would anyone pay for something they were already getting for free?" Geraldine shrugged and said how should *she* know? When no one else had questions, she returned to her seat.

Instead of having us move on from Current Events to religion the way we usually did on Monday mornings, Madame Frechette rose, caressed her front, and told us to *écoutez, s'il vous plaît*, because she had two important Current Event items of her own. Turning to the blackboard, she picked up a stick of chalk and wrote the words *remplaçante* and *tableaux vivants*.

"*Remplaçante*," she said, turning back to face us. "Any guesses?"

"Replacement?" someone said.

"*Oui. Très bien*. Replacement, or substitute." Madame explained that she would be taking the train home to Québec over the Thanksgiving holiday and so would not be in class on Wednesday for our half-day session. We would therefore have a *remplaçante*. Jackie Burnham reminded her that *she* was the *remplaçante*.

"*D'accord,*" Madame agreed. "And so, on Wednesday, you shall have a *remplaçante* for your *remplaçante,* heh heh heh. And, *mes élèves,* the Good Lord willing, I shall rejoin you all next Monday, one week from *aujourd'hui.*" Her saying it that way—"the Good Lord willing"—made me think of that movie we'd been watching when Sister Dymphna went cuckoo, *The Miracle of Marcelino.* One day you could be walking around like normal, and the next day your bed would be empty and God the Father's voice would be telling your family or whoever, "Sorry. I needed him in Heaven." Still, I wasn't too worried. Unless Madame's train got derailed near a cliff or something on her way back from Canada, I figured she'd be back after Thanksgiving like she said.

MaryAnn H. (not MaryAnn S. or MaryAnn V., the other two MaryAnns in our class) asked Madame who our sub was going to be, and Madame said she was quite sure it would be Sister Mary Agrippina. The entire class, minus Zhenya, who had yet to be ruler-slapped or skin-twistered, groaned. Madame shook a scolding finger at us, but she was smiling as she did so. "And now," she said, pointing to the other thing she'd written on the board. "Who can tell me what *tableau vivant* might mean?"

I recognized the term from Madame's report card and raised my hand. "Is it a tablecloth?" I asked.

"A tablecloth?" Madame Frechette looked puzzled. "*Non, non.*"

When nobody else said anything, Madame explained that *tableau vivant* meant a "living picture," and that our fifth grade class had been given a very special role in the upcoming Christmas program. Our class would present a series of four *tableaux vivants*, which would complement the musical interludes of St. Aloysius Gonzaga's eighth grade orchestra, seventh grade choir, sixth grade chorus, and fourth grade glee club. "But you, *mes amis*, will be the stars of the show!"

Madame assured us that she had had considerable experience as a director of theatricals back in her native province and even *un petit peu* of experience in the big city of Montreal, and that now she had been called upon to direct St. Aloysius Gonzaga's first-ever Christmas *tableaux*. Recalling Mother Filomina's "additional remarks" on Madame's report card, I thought I remembered not that she'd been "called upon" but that Madame had asked for this assignment and Mother Fil was *thinking* about it. "It will be very exciting," she promised now. "When the curtains part to reveal you all, *en costume* and as still as statues, depicting the various scenes of *l'histoire de la Nativité*, you will hear gasps of wonder from the audience!" There would be much to talk about, and much to do, upon our return from Thanksgiving break, but for now she could tell us that the four "living pictures" in which we would star would be the Annunciation, the shepherds' spotting of the Star of Bethlehem, the Wise Men's journey to see Baby Jesus, and the grand finale: a nativity which would include shepherds, angels, Magi, the Holy Family, of course, and last but not least, the little drummer boy, heh heh heh. (Here, Madame looked right at me.)

Hands flew up even before Madame stopped talking. *"Oui, monsieur?"*

"What about Santa Claus?" Monte Montoya asked.

"Non, non. Father Christmas was not in Bethlehem that night, heh heh heh, and so he will not be a part of our *tableaux."* Madame acknowledged Susan Ekizian. *"Oui, mademoiselle?"*

"Will there be animals?"

"Well, we shall have to see about that. Live animals? Most likely not. But put on your thinking caps, *mes amis.* How might we represent cows, sheep, donkeys, and camels?" Ernie Overturf said his father could maybe cut out some plywood animals with his table saw and Ernie could paint them. Madame clapped her hands and said that would be *magnifique.*

When Rosalie Twerski's hand went up, I knew what was coming "Can I be Mary?" she asked. Madame said she had made no decisions about casting yet, but that she would think about this over vacation and get back to us.

"What are we going to do for Baby Jesus?" Margaret Elizabeth McCormick wanted to know. She volunteered her three-month-old nephew.

Madame said she thought using an actual infant might present complications and that we would probably use a prop—a baby doll. Margaret Elizabeth said she had one of those, too. "*Et bien*. But more about our *tableaux vivants* later," Madame said. "For now, please take out your *livres mathématiques* so that we can see how successfully you have borrowed your fractions, heh heh."

Just as Madame had said, on the Wednesday half-day before Thanksgiving vacation, she was gone and there in her place sat the Enforcer, Sister Mary Agrippina, her hands folded in front of her, her scowl saying, *Just try something, anything and the pain I will inflict in return will make you wish you hadn't.*

Of course, none of this was obvious to Zhenya Kabakova who, midway through that morning, rose from behind her desk and, pencil in hand, walked toward the pencil sharpener on the other side of the room—a perfectly legal act in the classroom that Madame Frechette superintended, which, of course, was neither apparent nor acceptable to Sister Mary Agrippina. "Young lady!" she called out. "Just where do you think you're going?" In response, Zhenya held up her pencil.

Sister Mary Agrippina informed Zhenya that she did not read sign language and invited her to *say* what she thought she was doing.

Zhenya shrugged, looked around at the rest of us, and then turned back to Madame's substitute. "Pincil sharpenter," she said. "My pincil point ees dull." Sister Mary Ag rose from behind her desk and walked toward Zhenya. The rest of us geared up for the showdown.

Height-wise, Zhenya had Sister Mary Agrippina by at least three inches, and whereas our classmate was robust and muscular, her opponent had jowls and a considerable paunch. But if this was a match between David and Goliath, it was difficult to decide who was who.

"I guess I must have developed temporary amnesia," Sister said with a sarcastic smirk. "Because I can't recall having given you permission to get up and use the pencil sharpener."

"Don't need peermission," Zhenya countered. "What ees beeg deal you are making h'about thees?"

"The big deal?" said Sister. "The big deal is that you are being openly defiant, and *that*, young lady, is entirely unacceptable." She moved a step closer so that the two were face to face, separated by a scant few inches.

At which point Zhenya called upon one of the expressions that Lonny Flood had taught her. "Why not you go sheet een you het?" she said.

The rest of sat there frozen—a wide-eyed, horrified *tableau vivant*. All of us, that is, except Rosalie. "She just told you you should go to the bathroom in your hat, Sister," she said.

"Oh she did, did she?" Sister Mary Agrippina

said. Then she reared back and slapped Zhenya, hard as she could, across the face.

Zhenya looked stunned. She reached up and, with her right hand, rubbed her stinging cheek. Then she, too, reared back, formed a fist, and clocked Sister Mary Agrippina in the jaw, hard enough so that the old coot lost her balance and fell back against Eugene Bowen's desk. Attempting to get up, she fell back again, this time landing in Eugene's lap. Rosalie stood, ran toward the back door, and down to the office to tattle.

You'd have thought Zhenya's actions would have gotten her expelled, wouldn't you? Or, at least, suspended indefinitely? But that was not the case. The language barrier and cultural misunderstanding, not Zhenya, were blamed for the assault on Sister Mary Agrippina who, over the Thanksgiving interlude, got transferred from St. Aloysius Gonzaga Parochial School to some retirement home for Catholic sisters in Galilee, Rhode Island. I felt sorry for those old nuns if Sister Mary Ag was going to be taking care of them the way she took care of us, but I felt glad for my class and me. Zhenya had brought Sister Mary Gestapo's reign of terror to an end. And besides, maybe she only liked to torture kids.

When we returned to school the following Monday, other things had changed as well. Madame Frechette was wearing high heels with a leopard skin pattern, a new "poodle"-style hairdo, and a bright red beret, which she wore both outside of class and in. As director of the upcoming *tableaux vivants*, she also had a new, strictly business attitude. Lonny and Zhenya, over our four-and-a-half-day hiatus, had somehow become boyfriend and "geuhlfriend." About a third of our female classmates had returned from break wearing braids or pigtails. Three girls—two of the MaryAnns plus Nancy Whiteley—had tried conditioning their hair with mayonnaise and were now doing it on a regular basis. No fewer than seven girls had pierced their ears with little gold threads—"starters," they called them.

Even Rosalie Twerski had transformed herself. She showed up that Monday with shaved legs—the left one bearing Band-Aids in two different places, the right leg in three. Shockingly, she, too, had pierced her ears and was wearing tiny gold crucifixes on her punctured lobes. More shocking still, she had emerged from her mother's maroon Chrysler Newport that morning wearing a lime green Carnaby Street cap—and a bra! At first I assumed Rosalie was mocking Zhenya—that she had turned her into a belated Halloween costume. Then I took into account Turdski's fiercely competitive nature and realized what was really going on: if she could not defeat this foreign interloper whose popularity had soared into the stratosphere as a result of her having assaulted and banished the scourge of St. Aloysius, then she would try her damnedest to out-Zhenya her.

The race was on. The *tableau vivant* was upon us. The role of the Blessed Virgin Mary was up for grabs.

5

Meatloaf

Monday, December 7, 1964. I had awaited its arrival for weeks, little suspecting that it would become a day that would live in Felix Funicello infamy.

My classmates, too, had been anticipating the arrival of Monday, December the seventh, as Madame Frechette had told us this would be the day when, after Current Events and recess, she would announce her decisions about who would be who in our *tableaux vivants*. But for me, the casting of a Christmas program still two weeks away was of lesser importance than what would happen later that afternoon. I'd arrived at school that morning dressed not as a parochial school student but as a seafaring boy. (Boy Scouts, Girl Scouts, and Junior Midshipmen had permission to wear their uniforms to St. Aloysius on the days when they had after-school meetings.) During Current Events, my current event was that in six more hours I would board a bus to Hartford with my fellow Midshipmen and, at 4:00 P.M., appear on Channel 3's *Ranger Andy Show*. Over the weekend, I'd rung doorbells up and down our street to let neighbors know about my impending television debut and had made a sign for Pop to post at the lunch counter alerting our regulars. When I'd suggested that he might also want to lug our TV down to the lunch counter again and pass out more free pie, Pop had nixed that idea, claiming that more heavy lifting might give him a "sacroiliac attack" and that the last thing he needed was for our customers to get too used to free food.

"Ah," Madame noted. "First your mother was on *télévision*, and now you shall be, too, eh?"

"Yeah. Plus, my third cousin, Annette Funicello, has been on TV billions of times." Turning back to the class, I asked if there were any questions. Zhenya's hand went up. "Zhenya?"

"Who eez det? H'Annette Foony Jello?" (To Zhenya, I was Fillix Foony Jello, as in, while choosing sides at recess, "H'okay, I peeks Fillix Foony Jello.")

"Well, she used to be a Mouseketeer on TV and now she's a movie star."

"Ya? Movie star at seenima? Wow-ee, Fillix! You cousin beeg shut, ya?"

I nodded. "Anyone else?" Turdski's hand went up. "Rosalie?"

She wasn't at her desk; she was over at the first aid station by the pencil sharpener that had been set up for the girls whose pierced ears had gotten infected. "Just a sec," she said. Upturning the bottle of rubbing alcohol, she soaked a pair of cotton balls and applied them to her inflamed and oozy earlobes. Then, instead of asking me something about my current event like I thought she was going to, she turned to Zhenya and phony-smiled. "Zhenya, I just want to point out to you that it's pronounced 'cinema,' not 'seenima.' Like 'mortal or venial *sin*.' Say it: *ci*nema." From his seat in the back, Franz Duzio, who'd never quite mastered the art of whispering, wondered not-so-quietly who'd died and made *her* the teacher.

"Seenima," Zhenya said.

Rosalie shook her head. "*Sin* . . . ema. Try it again."

"*Seen* . . . ema."

"En . . . ema," someone mumbled. Giggles followed.

Rosalie smiled with patronizing patience and, turning to Madame, promised to work with Zhenya on her pronunciation during recess. Zhenya shook her head. "Uh uh. Nyet. At recess, I play bezbull or dujbull."

As a parochial school student, I was, of course, well acquainted with the story of Jesus's crucifixion and knew that a kiss or a sugary smile from a "friend" could be treacherous. And so, in defense of Zhenya, I smiled, too—at my nemesis. "Oh, that reminds me, Rosalie," I said. "It's 'picnic,' not 'pitnic.'"

Turdski's smile turned sour. "Yeah? So?"

"You always pronounce it 'pitnic.'"

"I do not!"

"Yeah, you do, Rose," one of the unassailable Kubiaks chimed in. Several of the boys nodded. Some of the girls might have nodded, too, had Rosalie not wielded so much power. Geraldine Balchunas sprang to the defense of her best friend. "If she says 'pitnic,' then how come *I* never heard her, and I go over to her house all the time?"

"*Et bien, mesdames and messieurs, ça suffit.* And now—"

Ignoring Geraldine and Madame, I kept my focus on Rosalie. "Repeat after me: I will bring potato salad to the class *pic . . . nic.*" Out of the corner of my eye, I saw Madame cover her grin with her hand.

"I'm not repeating anything," Turd Girl said. "I

know it's 'picnic,' so you can just shut up, *Dondi*." At this point, Madame intervened in earnest, reminding Rosalie that telling others to "shut up" in her classroom was grounds for a check-minus. Opening her grade book, she turned a deaf ear to Rosalie's argument that she hadn't *told* me to shut up; she'd merely said that I could shut up—if I wanted to. Madame rose and wrote the French spelling, *pique-nique*, on the board. To me she said, "Finish up now, *monsieur, s'il vous plait.*"

I nodded. "Any other questions?"

Geraldine was gunning for me now. "When you go on that show today, are you afraid you'll break the TV camera and have to pay for it because you're so ugly?" None of the boys laughed, but several girls did. Madame Frechette came to my defense—or tried to, anyway. I wish she hadn't. "That will be enough of that, *mademoiselle*. I am quite sure no cameras will be broken. And I'm sure you will all agree that *Monsieur Felix* looks quite dashing in his seaman's uniform."

Lonny's shocked whisper carried up from the back of the class. "What'd she just say then? Did she just say what I thought she said? Holy crap!" I didn't get why he was going so mental.

"Ah, recess time, *mes élèves*," Madame noted with a sigh of relief. "And *après votre récréation*, we shall discuss our *tableaux vivants*. Class dismissed!"

Some of the girls retrieved their jump ropes from the cloak room and others made for the rubbing alcohol and cotton balls. Us boys took bats, balls, and bases out of the closet and pushed past the girls and down the stairs.

"Hey," I said to Lonny on our way out of the building. "What'd you think Madame said back there?"

He guffawed. "Oh my god, don't you know what semen is?" I told him yeah—a seaman was a sailor. A squid. He shook his head and laughed even louder. "It's, you know, spunk."

"What's spunk?"

"Oh, man, Felix. Ain't you ever had a wet dream?"

Was he talking about bed-wetting? "Not since I was real little," I said. That made him laugh so hard that he dropped to his knees. I still didn't get it, but at least now I realized we were in the birds-and-the-bees ballpark. My ignorance was Pop's fault, of course. All's he'd told me about sex was that stuff about drinking fountains. If I was ever going to figure it all out, I'd just have to listen harder on the school bus— be Sherlock Holmes, kind of.

Out on the playground, everyone was talking about whether Rosalie or Zhenya would get picked to be Mary when we went back inside. Ever since we'd returned from Thanksgiving break, the class had divided itself, more or less, into two factions. Most of the girls wanted Rosalie and most of us boys wanted Zhenya. Both candidates, in their own way, had been campaigning for the part. Zhenya had taken out her braids and begun wearing her long brown hair (made lustrous with mayonnaise) down, and, I noticed, too, that she'd begun jacking up the volume when we prayed the rosary: "Blissid art dou kh'amongst vimmin and blissid eez duh froot uff die voomb." Rosalie had left an anonymous typewritten note on Madame's desk. (It *had* to have been her, although when Madame asked the writer to reveal him-or-herself, she hadn't owned up.) The note said how Communists were atheists, and how atheists had no right to celebrate Christmas. In addition to the note, Rosalie had taken to wearing a winter scarf to school—not wrapped around her neck but draped over her head like a veil. Lonny, who, in the Virgin Mary sweepstakes, was rooting for his "geuhlfriend," had at one point confronted potato-nosed Rosalie with the question, "How come you're wearing that stupid thing all the time now?" Rosalie had fake-coughed and claimed that she had a very, *very* bad head cold and that her mother had insisted she cover her head in our draughty classroom. "Yeah, right," Lonny scoffed. "You got a head cold and I'm the Leader of the Pack." With a laugh, he crouched into a motorcyclist's stance and made loud *rum-rum-rum* engine noises. Twerski's retort was that Lonny was the Leader of the Retards.

But if Rosalie's remark was inappropriate for a girl in the finals of the Blessed Virgin sweepstakes, then Zhenya's conduct out on the playground twenty minutes before Madame's big announcement that day was every bit as un-Marylike. Designated one of the day's baseball captains, I was making my picks when, unexpectedly, Father Hanrahan appeared on the opposite side of the playground where the hoop was, dribbling a basketball and wondering real loud who wanted to play some Twenty-One? "Me!" all us boys shouted, throwing down our gloves and running toward him. Father Hanrahan was the only cool person at St. Aloysius—he even let you call him Father Jerry if you felt like it—and his appearance on the playground was almost like having Bill Russell or John Havlicek show up. But though Zhenya loved both "bezbull" and "dujbull," she was indifferent to, and had no aptitude for, "bezgetbull." Separating herself from the rest of us, she glanced over at the jump-roping girls and then walked by herself to the fence. Lonny, older and taller than the rest of us, was the best basketball player in our class. "Hey!" I called to him as he walked toward Zhenya. "Aint you playing?"

"Nah."

A minute later, he had his arm around her. Two minutes after that, they were kissing, regular or French I couldn't see.

Jump ropes fell to the pavement and the girls clustered *en masse*, looking over toward the fence. Oblivious, Father Jerry and half of the boys were still playing Twenty-One, but the other half of us were staring in disbelief at Lonny and Zhenya, same as the girls. This was the most shocking thing our class had witnessed since Zhenya's socking of Sister Mary Agrippina. Glancing back at the building for a second, I saw that Sister Cecilia's third graders were crowded at their classroom windows, watching the show as well. I figured Sister Cecilia was probably out in the hall talking to Sister Godberta as usual. But if those two second-floor nuns were unaware of the passion on display, Mother Filomina was not. Her first-floor office window flew open with a bang, and she shook the bell harder than Ma shakes the thermometer before she sticks it in under my tongue when I'm sick. "Evgeniya Kabakova and the rest of the fifth grade girls should proceed immediately to the fire escape on the side of the building for an emergency class meeting with Sister Fabian!" she shouted. "Lonny Flood should come to the office, and any boy not playing basketball with Father should run laps around the school building. *Now!*"

When the recess bell rang, panting and sweaty from all those laps, I trudged up the stairs beside Zhenya, who looked both teary-eyed and defiant. "What was the emergency meeting about?" I whispered, as if I didn't already know. Instead of answering my question, Zhenya asked under her breath what those "guddamned pinguins" knew about "keesing boyzes." But at the drinking fountain, Susan Ekizian filled me in on the gist of the fire escape confab. Addressing all the fifth grade girls, but mostly looking and shaking her finger at Zhenya, Mother Fil had assured them that young ladies who kept themselves pure for their future husbands ran a better-than-even chance of meeting those husbands in the confession line, and that God would reward them with happy marriages and beautiful children. She likewise had warned that any girl who made herself "the occasion of sin for a boy" just might be purchasing a one-way ticket to Hell. The meeting had closed with a recitation of the Catholic Legion of Decency pledge to embrace virtue and to resist lustful behavior and condemned movies.

Back in class, Madame was missing and the girls were abuzz about how Rosalie, beyond a doubt, now had a lock on the role of the Blessed Virgin Mary in our *tableaux vivants*. What were they doing with Lonny, I wondered. Torturing him? Making him sit across from Monsignor Muldoon and read that Saint Aloysius Gonzaga booklet? Not out loud, I hoped—Lonny wasn't too hot at reading aloud. But when I got up to sharpen my pencil, I saw Lonny back outside again with Father Hanrahan. Father was doing most of the talking, and Lonny's head kept going up and down in agreement with whatever he was saying. Plus, they kept bounce-passing the basketball between them. Then Father stopped talking and they began playing one on one.

Madame returned, smelling like cigarettes and freshly applied lily-of-the-valley perfume. I had assumed she would simply announce her *tableaux vivants* decisions, but she'd prepared in advance while we were at recess. The world map had been pulled down and, with a bit of dramatic flair, Madame approached it and gave it a yank. "*Voilà!*" she said. Our *tableaux* assignments were revealed on the blackboard beneath.

Most of Madame's decisions were shockers, with two exceptions. I had been cast as the Little Drummer Boy in the nativity scene and Marion Pemberton, the only colored kid in our class, was to be the only colored Wise Man. But Franz Duzio, with his eight million detentions, as the Angel Gabriel? Lonny

Flood as Joseph? Most shocking of all, neither Rosalie Twerski nor Zhenya Kabakova would be the Blessed Virgin Mary; both had been assigned the roles of lowly shepherdesses. Casting against type, Madame had chosen shy, chubby, cat's-eye-glasses-wearing Pauline Papelbon to play the Virgin. "Sister Mary Potato Chips," some of the mean girls in our class had dubbed Pauline because of her fondness for Ripples, Cheetos, Fritos, and Flings. I turned from the board to my fellow classmates. Zhenya looked indifferent. Rosalie looked outraged. Pauline Papelbon snuck something from her desk and put it in her mouth. I thought I glimpsed the trace of a smile.

Whereas my mother's humiliation had been televised nationally, *Ranger Andy* was only a local program. Still, part of my excitement about my TV appearance that afternoon was rooted in my desire to vindicate Ma. I would erase the memory of her Pillsbury Bake-Off disaster with my own televised triumph. Kids who were guests at the Ranger Station sat together in three rows of bleacher seats, but Ranger Andy frequently needed helpers. If, say, a magician was a featured guest, a kid with quick hand-raising reflexes might be chosen to step to the front of the room and become a magician's assistant. A zoologist from the science museum might need a kid to come on up, pet the snake coiled around his arm, and verify that its skin was smooth and cool to the touch, not rough and scaly. And, of course, whatever the needs of that day's featured guest, there was the daily need for a volunteer to carry the Ranger Station's mail pouch up to the front so that Ranger Andy could pull out a letter or two and answer questions that kids had written in to ask.

I was the only St. Aloysius Gonzaga student in my Junior Midshipmen corps. (To join, you had to have a father who'd been in the U.S. Navy like Pop, or the Coast Guard or the Sea Bees.) The other kids in our company—the two Michael M's (Morosky and Morrison), Howie Slosberg, Peter Goldberg,

Denny Dermody, Marty Andreadis, Terrence Evashevski, and Danny Baldino—all went to public school. (Or, as Lonny called it, "pubic" school.)

Poor Danny. On the ride up to Hartford, he got bus-sick and puked all over his uniform, and everyone else was holding their nose and saying *they* were gonna puke, too, from smelling it and looking at it. Mr. Dean and Mr. Agnello had to have the bus driver stop at a gas station so's they could go in the bathroom and help Danny clean up or else he couldn't be on the show. And while they were in there, the rest of us started singing, "A Hundred Bottles of Beer on the Wall." We were on either eighty-nine or eighty-eight bottles of beer when the bus driver turned psycho. He got up and yelled at us to all shut up or else he was gonna turn the bus around and take us home without ever going on *Ranger Andy*. So everyone shut up and looked down at our shoes. And by the time Mr. Agnello and Mr. Dean got back on the bus with Danny—the front of his uniform was soaked from getting the puke off—the bus driver wasn't acting psycho anymore. He shifted into gear and continued on to Hartford.

Hartford was big and it had tall buildings and traffic jams. Getting to the studio, the bus was moving like two inches an hour, but we still got there in time and the driver pulled open the door and all of us got out. The TV station was in this big glass building that had about four billion different floors. All of us squeezed into an elevator that had an elevator guy in a red uniform who had this skinny little mustache, and while he was taking us up to our floor, he was whistling. And you could still sorta smell Danny Baldino's uniform, even though it had gotten cleaned off. *I* could, anyways, cause I was squashed in right next to him. And the front of his uniform was still kinda wet, even though, on the bus, Mr. Agnello had pulled open the window where Danny was sitting so's it could get some fresh air and dry out, and Danny's teeth had chattered and his lips had turned kinda blue because it was pretty cold out—cold enough for everyone except Danny to be wearing our Junior Midshipmen pea coats.

Inside the studio, this director guy had us practice walking in and sitting down when, later, we heard Ranger Andy say, "Who's that coming down the trail?" and he told us about how, when we said our names, a microphone was going to move over our heads but that we should look straight ahead at Ranger Andy and not up at the microphone because people watching us on TV wouldn't see the micro-phone and would go, "Why are those kids all looking up?" There were two other groups who were gonna be on the show with us, a Girl Scout troop, plus some kids from some Hebrew school. We all sat down on the bleachers (us Junior Midshipmen were in the back row), and the lights were so bright that they almost made you blind, and so hot that I was boiling to death in my uniform. On TV the Ranger Station looked like a log cabin, but in person it was real fake and made out of cardboard, not real wood, and even Ranger

Andy's *desk* wasn't wood, it was whatchamacallit—particleboard, that Pop says is real cheap-o.

When Ranger Andy came out, he was pretty nice but older than he looked on TV and kinda wrinkly. *And* he had makeup on. Rouge, over what Ma called "five o'clock shadows." And these kinda yellowy teeth. He told us that when the show started, we had to be real quiet and pay attention because it was "live," and if we talked out of turn, it would make the show stink. (He didn't *say* "stink," but that's what he meant.) When he asked who wanted to bring the mail bag up during the show, both me and Michael Morosky were the first ones to raise our hands, and Ranger Andy looked right at me and I thought he was gonna pick me, but then he picked Michael instead.

Besides us and the other two groups of kids, Ranger Andy's guest was this guy and his pet raccoon that he'd tamed, and the raccoon's name was Felix. Which all the other Junior Midshipmen thought was funny, but I didn't.

Then the director guy went, "Three, two, one . . . and we're on!"

First, Ranger Andy played his banjo and sang the Ranger Station song, which I knew the words to, on account of I get to watch *Ranger Andy* if my sisters aren't home from high school yet, except when they *are* home, it's two against one, so they get to watch *their* boring show, *Bandstand,* and dance with each other. (When they slow-dance, Simone's always the girl and Frances is always the boy and gets to lead.) But anyways, this is how the Ranger Station song goes. It goes:

My name is Ranger Andy and I've traveled all around
And I will tell you many things about the things I've
   found
I'll sing about the mysteries of animals galore
And hope to show you many things you've never seen
   before
Come along, sing a song, da da da da da da da da
   (I forgot that part.)

After Ranger Andy sang the Ranger Station song, he said, "Who's that coming down the trail?" so we all walked in and sat down, and then that microphone moved over our heads and we all said our names, except most kids forgot that they weren't supposed to look up, but I didn't. I looked right at Ranger Andy like they said to do, and Ranger Andy was probably going to himself, Jeeze, I should have picked *that* kid to bring up the mail bag cause he really pays attention.

They showed this movie where beavers were building a beaver dam, and a *Farmer Alfalfa* cartoon where the mice shoot off a cannon and it makes the cat go bald. Then the guy with the raccoon came out. He asked who wanted to feed Felix and all the other Junior Midshipmen looked at me and kinda laughed. One of the Girl Scouts got picked. And guess what she got to feed Felix? This empty ice cream cone with no ice cream in it, and he sat up on his hind legs and held the cone between his paws and ate like *crunch, crunch, crunch*. It was pretty funny. Then Michael brought the mail bag up and Ranger Andy opened some of the letters from kids and answered their questions like what was his favorite river and did Old Faithful ever *not* erupt when it was supposed to? Then Mr. Agnello told Ranger Andy some stuff about what Junior Midshipmen was, and the Girl Scout lady said stuff about the Girl Scouts, and this guy, Rabbi somebody, who was wearing one of those little beanies like "Cowboy" Zupnik down at the lunch counter wears, talked about what kids learn in Hebrew school. And during a commercial, the director guy told Ranger Andy that they were running ahead of schedule and he should stretch it because they had two extra minutes to kill. So after the commercial, Ranger Andy asked did anyone have any jokes they wanted to tell?

Danny Baldino (whose uniform was dry by then) told an elephant joke that was like: How can you tell when an elephant's been in your refrigerator? I don't know. How? Because you can see his footprints in the butter.

And this Hebrew school kid went, "Why is it impossible to starve in the desert?" And Ranger Andy said he didn't know. Why? And the kid went, "Because of all the *sand which is* there." Ranger Andy said that was a good one.

Then he looked over at the director and the director made this stretching move with his hands like that guy who makes salt water taffy down at Ocean Beach. So Ranger Andy said, "Looks like we have time for one more. Anyone else have a joke?" And I was the only one who raised my hand, so he picked me.

"How is a lady like a stove?" I asked.

"Hmm, you got me," Ranger Andy said. "How?"

When I said the answer, nobody laughed and one of the kids in the Hebrew school row went, "Whoa!" Ranger Andy looked for a couple of seconds like he forgot where he was. Then he looked over at the director and the director was doing this thing where it looked like he was karate-chopping himself in the throat. Then all those hot lights went off.

On the bus ride back, nobody said much and nobody wanted to sit next to me, except Mr. Dean sat with me for a few minutes and I was like, "How was *I* supposed to know it was a dirty joke?" and trying not to cry. And that night, Mr. Agnello and Ma talked for a real long time on the phone, and Ma kept saying how I certainly didn't hear a joke like that at *our* house because no one in our family ever talked like that.

The next day at school wasn't as bad as I thought it was going to be. Madame didn't say anything, and neither did any of the nuns. I'd been kinda worried that they were going to make me have another talk with Monsignor Muldoon, but I was also kinda hoping that Father Jerry might take me out on the playground to have the talk and maybe him and me would shoot some baskets. But neither of those things happened. None of the kids in my class said anything snotty about what I'd said on TV, not even

Rosalie. I thought it was because her and everyone else was still so hepped up about the *tableaux vivants*, but then later on Oscar Landry told me it was because, when Madame made me bring that note down to the office first thing in the morning, she warned everyone that if anyone made fun of me about what had happened, she was giving them not just *one* check-minus but *two*. The only kid who said anything mean was this dumbo sixth grader who, out on the playground, came up to me and said, didn't I think meatloaf was so-oooo delicious? But that was it. Oh, and Lonny? He said he thought that, because of me, it was the best *Ranger Andy* show he'd ever seen, and that for once it wasn't boring.

And this was weird: after school? After I got home? I put *Ranger Andy* on, except they made this announcement that, due to something-something circumstances, the Ranger Station was closed until further notice. And instead, they showed this real old program called *Boston Blackie*. Boston Blackie was this detective guy who had a real skinny mustache like that elevator operator at the TV station up in Hartford, and he looked like him, too, so it might have even been the same guy, but maybe not. I'm not sure.

6

Drama

Madame's decision not to cast Rosalie as the Blessed Virgin in our *tableau* carried repercussions, as I discovered the afternoon Madame made me stay after school for making cross-eyes at Arthur Coté to try and make him laugh instead of doing my silent reading. I was on the last six or seven of my hundred sentences she was making me write—*I shall not distract my neighbors*—when the four of them appeared at the back door of Madame's classroom: Rosalie, her parents, and

Mother Filomina. *"Bonjour, bonjour,"* Madame called back to them. "Thank you for coming." She slipped her feet back into her leopard-spotted high heels, adjusted the angle of her red beret, and swallowed noticeably. Then she rose and walked back to join the lynching party—hers.

I couldn't hear everything that was being said, just bits and pieces—the kind of information you picked up by eavesdropping in the confession line.

Mother Filomina: "I think we can all appreciate that Mrs. Frechette is newly arrived and might not necessarily..."

Mrs. Twerski: "...is, I'm sure, a lovely young lady, but from what I've heard—and I hope I'm not telling tales out of school—her overeating most likely stems from the fact that her mother is very unstable *emotionally.*"

Rosalie: "I just feel that the smartest kid and the hardest worker in our whole class should get to..."

Mr. Twerski: "And as usual, Twerski Impressions

will be printing the program free of charge, with a *three*-color cover this year. *And* we're . . ."

Mother Filomina again: "Three dozen reams of mimeograph paper! My stars, with our budget as tight as it is, we're so grateful for this generous . . ."

Mrs. Twerski again: ". . . Sister Mary Agrippina having been transferred after the incident with that awful Russian girl. . . . And speaking not so much as an Advisory Board member but as a parent, it seems to me that if you're at all *interested* in the permanent substitute's position, you'd be a very viable . . ."

Rosalie again: "Please, Madame. *Pleeease.*"

I could tell they had poor Madame on the ropes, and since when was four against one a fair fight? Putting the last period at the end of my one hundredth *I shall not distract my neighbors* sentence, I grabbed my paper, cleared my throat, and walked back there. "Finished," I said.

Madame took my paper. "*Et bien*, Felix. Then you may go now."

I hesitated, scuffing the toe of my shoe against the floorboard. "Could I say something first?"

Rosalie shook her head. "This is a private meeting, in case you didn't notice, Felix. Mind your own beeswax."

"Now, sweetheart," her mother said. Mother Filomina asked me what I wished to say. I didn't know, really. I just wanted to stop the bullying.

"Just that I think Madame Frechette . . . as a teacher . . . is *magnifique!*"

Madame's eyes blinked back tears. "*Merci bien*," she said.

I nodded. Asked her if, before I left, did she want her boards wiped down and her erasers clapped? Madame said she would like that very much. Rosalie rolled her eyes.

Maybe it was the power of her leopard-spotted shoes and red beret, or my having just proclaimed her magnificence. Or maybe Madame hated Rosalie's guts the same as me. Whatever it was, by the end of

their meeting, she still had not yielded to the Twerskis' and Mother Filomina's full-court press. What
she offered, instead, was *un accommodement*—a compromise. Pauline Papelbon would retain the role of
the Virgin Mary; Madame did not have the heart to
snatch the role away from the poor girl, she said. But
if Rosalie didn't mind a bit of cross-gender casting,
she could be upgraded from a shepherdess to a king.
"Caspar, Melchior, or Balthasar, *mademoiselle.* You may
have your pick, as I'm sure any of the boys would be
happy to become a shepherd instead of a Wise Man."
(The Kubiak brothers, through their 4-H contacts,
had offered live lambs for our grand finale. Madame
had vacillated for a while but finally had surrendered
to our pleas.) "Now which of the Magi might you
wish to be?"

"Not the colored one," Rosalie blurted. I saw
Mother Filomina wince a little, and Rosalie must
have seen it, too. "Because Marion Pemberton said
he really, really wants to be that one and so I think

he should." This, of course, was what Zhenya Kabakova would classify as "boolsheet." Marion wanted to be a shepherd just as much as the rest of us boys.

"Well, let me put it another way," Madame said. "What gift would you like to present to the Christ child: gold, frankincense, or myrrh?"

Mr. Twerski answered for his daughter. "What the hay, honey? Go for the gold." Which meant that Turdski would be Caspar and Eugene Bowen was going to give up his crown in exchange for one of those live lambs, the lucky duck, and all's I was gonna get to hold was my stupid *pa-rumpa-pum-pum* drum.

After they left, I heard Madame's sigh all the way from the back of the classroom. She was holding a tissue in her hand and looking out the window. I was pretty sure she was crying. "Well," I said. "The blackboards are done and I clapped the erasers. I guess I'll go now."

"And I will erase your check-minus for bothering Arthur," she said. Then she turned toward me, daubing her eyes and smiling. *"Monsieur Dondi,"* she said.

"Merci beaucoup." She approached me, shook my hand, and then leaned forward and kissed me on the forehead the same way Ma sometimes did. I sneezed all the way down the stairs.

As it turned out, the recasting of Rosalie as Caspar did not placate her. (Nor did she find it amusing when, as we walked side by side in the boys' and girls' lines on the way down to the lunchroom, I began singing, *"Caspar, the friendly ghost, the friendliest ghost you know..."*) Determined by hook or crook to be the star of the Saint Aloysius Gonzaga Christmas program, Turdski sat down that weekend and wrote a play, which, on Monday, she submitted directly to Mother Filomina and Sister Fabian, having bypassed Madame Frechette. Rosalie's script was so pukily worshipful that Mother Fil exulted even *before* Turdski claimed to have felt the hand of God pushing her ballpoint pen across the page as she wrote it. As a result of her experience,

Rosalie said, she was now considering a life of Holy Orders.

But if Saint Aloysius's Sisters of Charity were taken in by Rosalie's fake piety, Madame Frechette was not. As director of our *tableaux vivants*, she now had a competing impresario—one of her very own students. Madame was not pleased. *Her* players would be required merely to stand in place as the curtains opened, mute and still as statues, with the exception of a miscellaneous twitch or nervous tic. In contrast, Rosalie's actors—her faithful disciple Geraldine, the browbeaten Ernie Overturf, and a somewhat indignant Marion Pemberton—were free to speak, move about, and if need be, scratch an itch.

It wasn't an out-in-out battle between Rosalie and Madame; it was more like a tug of war. When Rosalie asked Madame if, instead of discussing our religion chapter, she and her actors could sequester themselves in the cloakroom for the purpose of practicing her play, Madame said *non*.

"Why not?" Rosalie asked. "It's religious."

"Why not? Because I *said* so, *mademoiselle*, that's why not," Madame said, in a tone of voice so contentious that, if you'd closed your eyes, you might have thought Sister Mary Agrippina had returned. A few minutes later, Rosalie said she had a headache and could she go see the nurse? And whether or not she really checked in with Nurse Gadle, it was obvious that she'd checked in with Sister Fabian, the assistant principal. The note she returned with, signed by Sister, gave her and her players permission to proceed to the lunch room on an as-needed basis during the ten o'clock religious instruction hour for the purpose of rehearsing "Jesus Is the Reason for the Season" for the upcoming Christmas program.

"*Et bien,*" Madame said through clenched teeth after she read the note.

But the following day she retaliated. Madame handed Ronald Kubiak her car keys and had Ronald, Oscar Landry, Eugene B., and me go out to her car, open her trunk, and bring back the boxes of Christmas decorations she'd brought in from home: wreaths with fake holly, strings of lights, a garland, a ceramic tree. There was a crèche in there, a plastic Santa Claus, some blow-up vinyl reindeer, a dozen or so Styrofoam candy canes with hooks at the top for hanging up. "We must make room for Christmas!" Madame declared just before we started our silent reading of the next-to-last *Yearling* chapter. And while the others read, I watched an energized Madame circulate about the room, yanking down the dozen or so posters that Rosalie had made for extra credit. When I looked over at Rosalie, I saw that she, too, was watching Madame, her nostrils aflare and her hands gripping *The Yearling* so tightly that her knuckles had turned bone white. "Madame Frechette?" she finally said. To which Madame responded, "Silent reading means just that, *mademoiselle*. Continue reading *en silence!*"

"Aplomb" was one of our vocabulary words that week, and after lunch, when we had to use all our vocab words in sentences, I wrote, "Madame took down all of Rosalie's posters with <u>aplomb</u>." The next day, when I got my paper back, Madame had written beside that sentence, *"Monsieur, vous êtes un fripon!"* Later, I looked up *fripon* in the big French-English dictionary in the bookcase and it said, "A rascal or rapscallion; one who is playfully mischievous."

Out on the playground at recess that day, Rosalie began organizing a grade-wide game of Octopus, Octopus, Cross My Sea. But Zhenya, who'd played Octopus once before, said, "Thet stoopit game for stoopit pipples. C'mun, Fillix. Go beck to clissroom and get bezbull gluff and I throw some grounders end flyink bulls for you ken prictiss." Lonny was absent that day, which was probably why Zhenya wanted me and her to hang around. I told her nah, I didn't really feel like it. The truth was, I liked playing Octopus, Octopus and was pretty good at it, too. Laughing, Zhenya reached over and jabbed me in the ribs. "C'mun, Fillix Foony Jello. You need prictiss. You throw and ketch bezbull just like leetle geuhl." To demonstrate, she did a comical version of the way I threw and caught. I tried not to laugh but couldn't help it; her imitation was pretty funny. "C'mun, Fil-lix, pliss. I titch you gooder than Meeky Mentels of New H'York H'Yinkees."

I told her okay, but when I asked Sister Scholas-tica, the teacher on playground duty, if I could go back in the building for my glove, she said no. So Zhenya and I ended up just walking around the school yard and talking.

"Can I ask you something?" I said.

"There is saying in Soviet Union," she said. "Esk me no kestyuns, I tell you no lice." Then she said she was only kidding. What did I want to ask her?

"Are you an atheist?"

"Ateist? No beleef in Gud? Nyet. I em Russian Or-todux." Which, she said, was close to "Rummin Ca-toleek." She made the sign of the cross and shrugged. "No Ortodux skool here, so I comes to Catoleek skool. H'okay?"

I nodded. "Can I ask you something else?"

"Ya ya, Meester Kestyun Man," she said. "Vut ilse you need to know?"

"How come you and your parents picked here to live?"

They hadn't at first, she said. When they'd first moved to America, they'd lived in Washington, D.C. "Just for month or so. Then we come to Kennede-kett. We come for my mama's verk."

I asked her, didn't she mean for her *father's* work?

"Nyet. My fodder ees writer. He can verk enny-vares. But not my mama."

"What does she do?" I asked.

"She engineer. H'okay?"

I shrugged. "Sure." Why was she asking me?

"So why did you guys leave Russia, anyways?" I asked.

To which Zhenya responded, once again, this time not grinning, "Esk me no kestyuns, I tell you no lice." Recovering her smile, she said, "Come on, Fillix, I change mind. Let's play dumb end stupit Octopus gemm." But when we walked over there, Rosalie said the game was already well underway and we couldn't just jump in—it wasn't fair.

"H'okay," Zhenya said. "No beeg dill, Rosalie *blyad'* geuhl." Turdski wanted to know what *that* was supposed to mean, to which Zhenya answered, "For me to know, for you note to know. And thees for you, too." Turning her back on Turdski, she bent over and wiggled her fanny at her. In response, Rosalie halted the game and ran to inform Sister Scholastica. While she was gone, Zhenya cupped her hand at the side of her mouth and whispered, "Just now? I call her slut geuhl."

"What's that?" I asked.

"Geuhl who, you knows, Fillix, opens hair legs for boyzes. Like, how you say? Prusteetoot."

"Oh," I said. "A chicky-boom boom."

She laughed. "Ya, ya. Cheeky-bum bum geuhl."

Sister Scholastica told Rosalie she could do nothing about what Zhenya had done because she hadn't witnessed the act herself, and that Rosalie should just go back and play. Poor Sister had better watch it, I thought. Next thing she knew, she'd be sitting in some stupid meeting with the Twerskis.

*　*　*

The next morning, while I was eating my Cheerios and finishing my homework sheet on gerunds, I glanced over at the newspaper. Only eight more shopping days till Christmas, it said. Later that morning, in social studies, we finished the Middle Ages. Madame said we would not move on to *la Renaissance* until after vacation. During arithmetic, we took our chapter test on fractions and in reading we finished *The Yearling*. (Flag croaked at the end, same as my purple Easter chick, Popeye, only at least I didn't have to shoot Popeye in the head the way Jody had to shoot his deer so's he could both put him out of his misery and become a man.) With all these pre-vacation wrap-ups, and only a week left before the big Christmas program, we started spending less and less time on schoolwork and more and more time on our *tableaux vivants*.

Via a letter each of us carried home the week before, Madame had assigned our parents homework:

they were supposed to buy or make us our costumes if they could (except for the angels, whose
costumes would be on loan from Careen of Careen's
Costume Shop, who was friends with MaryAnn Vocatura's mother.) Because Chino Molinaro had come
down with the flu, Ma was pinch-hitting for him at
the lunch counter with Pop, so she handed over the
costuming assignment to Simone, who was the most
theatrically inclined of any of us Funicellos anyways,
not counting Annette. And since Lonny had been
assigned the pivotal role of Joseph and his mother, as
usual, had shirked *her* responsibility, Simone agreed
to outfit him as well.

In my opinion, Simone was not that successful in
costuming me as the little drummer boy. With my
shorts, knee socks, and tricorn hat, I looked more
like Johnny Tremain than a boy from Bethlehem.
For my drum, Simone covered one of Ma's hat boxes
with contact paper, poked holes in the sides, and
threaded it with yarn so's it could hang down in

front of me. My souvenir chopsticks from China Village, where we'd gone after Frances's eighth grade graduation, would do as drumsticks, Simone said.

As for her dressing Lonny as Joseph of Nazareth, the summer before, Simone had caught the bouquet at our cousin Anna Ianuzzi's wedding and then had had to sit on a folding chair while Anna's creepy cousin Frido stretched this blue garter over her foot and halfway up her leg. Now she stretched that very same garter over Lonny's head, which she had covered with one of our striped dish towels. My blue terrycloth bathrobe, which went down past my knees, looked more like a tunic on Lonny. Simone had me go out to our garage and get the pushbroom. Then she had Lonny unscrew the broom part. After he'd done it, she handed him the handle and told him that was his staff. Lonny was good to go as Joseph, Simone said, except for his feet. On the day of the *tableaux*, she said, he would have to wear sandals or flip-flops, not his high-top Keds. Lonny said he thought there were some flip-flops in his father's closet from before he left to go to work in Florida as a fisherman. I didn't say anything when he said that, and neither did Simone, but we both kinda looked at each other for a second. We knew from our Uncle Bruno that Lonny's father was in prison in New York, not in Florida on some fishing boat.

On the Wednesday before the big Christmas program, we all got copies of Rosalie's play whether we wanted one or not. Her father had printed them on fancy paper at Twerski Impressions. After Rosalie passed them out, she made Ernie, Geraldine, and Marion read their parts. It was raining that morning, which meant indoor recess—unsupervised, for the most part, while Madame went off to the teachers' room. This was Rosalie's stupid play.

Jesus Is the Reason
for the Season

by Rosalie Elaine Twerski

CAST

Saint Aloysius Gonzaga . . . . . . Ernest Overturf

Saint Teresa of Lisieux . . . Geraldine Balchunas

Saint Martin de Porres . . . . . . Marion Pemberton

Narrator . . . . Miss Rosalie Elaine Twerski

The narrator comes out first. She is dressed in a pretty gown and wears lipstick, eye shadow, and a crown. She is very beautiful.

NARRATOR:

Hello. I am your narrator and this is a play about the true meaning of Christmas. We are up in Heaven where it is always beautiful and peaceful for the people who were good when they were alive. Hey, look. Here come some saints. Shhh. Let's listen.

SAINT ALOYSIUS:

Hello. I am Aloysius Gonzaga. I lived in Venice Italy when I was alive, but I died from the plague. Before I died, though, I was nice to children and lepers, and whenever I climbed up or down a set of stairs, I said the "Hail Mary" on every step. So God made me the patron saint of youth. And someday in the United States, which hasn't even been discovered yet except for the Indians, a wonderful Catholic school will be named after me because I was so nice and helpful to everyone. Hey, look. Here comes Saint Teresa of Lisieux. That's in France.

SAINT TERESA:

Hi, my name is Saint Teresa of Lisieux, but lots of people call me Teresa the Little Flower because I am very fragile—as delicate as a little wildflower in the forest. I loved God so much that to show Him my love, I would sleep under a heavy blanket in summer and not use any blanket in the winter when it was freezing cold, and if a fly or mosquito landed on me, I would not shoo it away because I wanted to offer my suffering to God. I was born in 1873 and died from tuberculosis in 1897. If you subtract 1873 from 1897, you get 24, which was pretty young for me to die. By the way, I am the patron saint of florists and airplane pilots. Oh, look who's coming. It's Martin de Porres, the only colored person to ever become a saint.

SAINT MARTIN:

Yes, it is me, Martin de Porres, the patron saint of mulattos and hairdressers. I can cure people with miracles. I heal them just by shaking their hand. And when I pray for poor people, my prayers are so strong that they make me glow in the dark. And I love animals so much that I even like rats and feel sorry for them when they can't get enough to eat. I wasn't made a saint until last year, 1963. And when I became a saint, I was so happy. But today I am very, very sad. Oh, I forgot to tell you. I was born in Peru, which is in South America.

NARRATOR:

So the saints start talking to each other.

SAINT TERESA:

Why are you so sad even though you're in Heaven, Saint Martin de Porres? Is it because prejudiced people are so mean to colored people?

SAINT MARTIN:

No, that's not it.

SAINT ALOYSIUS:

Are you sad because you like animals so
much, and if dogs have to go to the dog pound
and nobody claims them, they get put to sleep?

SAINT MARTIN:

No, that's not it either.

SAINT TERESA:

Oh, I think I know. You are unhappy
because Jewish people think Jesus was a very
nice man but not God. Is that it?

SAINT MARTIN:

No, that is not the reason why I am so
unhappy.

NARRATOR:

Saint Martin de Porres puts his hands over
his face and starts to cry.

SAINT TERESA:

Then tell us, Martin de Porres, why are you so sad that you are crying? Maybe we can help you.

SAINT MARTIN:

I am sad because all the children around the world have forgotten the true meaning of Christmas. All they care about is leaving cookies and milk for Santa so they can get presents under their tree and get their stockings stuffed with treats. They have forgotten that Christmas is a celebration of the birth of Baby Jesus, the Son of God. It is not about candy canes and wanting stuff from the store and having a big Christmas dinner with all your relatives. It is not about Christmas vacation where you don't have to do any homework for over a week. Christmas is about Jesus in the manger.

SAINT TERESA AND SAINT ALOYSIUS
TOGETHER:

You are right, Martin de Porres. Jesus is the
reason for the season.

SAINT ALOYSIUS:

Hey, I have an idea. Let's travel all around
the world and remind all the kids that Christmas is about the birth of the Christ child in
Bethlehem.

SAINT MARTIN:

But how will we travel around the world,
Saint Aloysius? We live in olden times before jet
planes and airlines like TWA were invented.
Oh, oh, what shall we do?

SAINT TERESA:

Hey, I know. Let's get a ride with Santa and
his reindeer. When they go around delivering
presents to children all over the world, we can

go down the chimney, too, and deliver our
message about Baby Jesus being the real reason
why we celebrate Christmas.

SAINT ALOYSIUS:

That is a great idea, Saint Teresa!

SAINT MARTIN:

Yes, let us go get ready. It is almost Christmas Eve.

NARRATOR:

And so the three saints rode all night long
with Santa in his sleigh, delivering their
important message. And on Christmas morning,
all the kids in the whole wide world, before they
went downstairs and opened their presents, knelt
and said their prayers and thanked God the
Father for sending His only son down to Earth
so that he could be born in Bethlehem with Mary
as his mother and Joseph as his stepfather, even

though the inn keeper was so mean to them that he made them sleep in a stable. And everyone was happy, except for atheists and Jewish people who don't believe that Jesus was the Son of God and so they only get to have Hanukkah where they light candles and get just small presents like shampoo and yo-yos and things like that, and they can't have a Christmas tree either.

The End.

After the read-through, I raised my hand. "Felix?" Rosalie said, her eyes squinting with suspicion. I told her I liked her play okay, but that the end didn't make sense.

"Yes, it does," she said. "Why doesn't it?"

"Because nobody in fifth grade still believes in Santa. How can they ride around the world with someone who doesn't really exist?"

Geraldine intervened. "Because they're saints, stupid. So they can fly."

"*Angels* can fly," I retorted. "No one ever said saints can."

Several classmates entered into the argument about whether or not saints could fly, and then Mary-Ann Haywood pointed out, reasonably enough, I thought, that the younger kids in our school still believed in Santa, and so for their sake, Rosalie could have the three saints travel with him in his sleigh on Christmas Eve so's it wouldn't wreck their innocence.

"Okay," I said. "But I still think it's kind of a dumb ending."

"Not as dumb as you are," Rosalie noted.

Then Marion Pemberton said he was quitting Rosalie's play. "You *can't* quit," Rosalie informed him. "You're the only one in our class who can play Martin de Porres."

"Why?" he shot back. "Because I'm black?" He made the point that Rosalie was playing one of the Three Kings in the *tableaux*. So if a female could play a male, why couldn't some white kid play a black saint? In return, Rosalie pointed out that Marion was also the black Wise Man in the *tableaux* and that *that* didn't bother him. "Yeah," he said, "but in your play, I have to cry, and I ain't crying in front of my father and my brothers Marvin and Roscoe and a whole bunch of other people that I don't even know." Rosalie made a big show of counting to ten with just her lips, no sound, and then she blew out this long, slow breath and said okay, all right already, he didn't have to cry. He could just look real, real sad. "*Okay?*" Reluctantly, Marion agreed.

When Madame returned, she let us get drinks and go to the toilet. Coming out of the boys' room, Lonny and I ran into Zhenya coming out of the girls' room. I asked them both what they thought of Rosalie's play.

"I think it's cornier than corn on the cob," Lonny said.

"I theenk eese sheetier than sheet," Zhenya said. "And I theenk, too, Rosalie ees *zhopalís*."

"What's that?" Lonny and I both asked.

"*Zhopalís?* Means peerson who gets nose brown from . . . how you say here sheet vit plinty vauter?"

"Diarrhea," I volunteered, thinking of poor Ma at the big Bake-Off.

"Ya, ya. Gets nose brown from direeya so det everyone theenk she good, good geuhl when she rilly just, how you say? I heered on TV last night: funny blunny." Lonny and I looked at each other and shrugged.

It wasn't until we were back in the classroom, starting science, that I realized Zhenya had called Rosalie exactly what she was: a brown-noser and a phony baloney.

After the Christmas program, Madame explained, each grade was going to invite their guests back to their own classrooms for refreshments. So all of us were supposed to go home and, for homework, find out what our mothers were making. The next day, she called us each by name and, when we told her what our mothers had said, she wrote it down.

The Kubiaks were bringing milk from their farm:

five gallons, plus paper cups. Arthur Coté was bringing three cans of Hawaiian Punch and a can opener. Pauline Papelbon said she'd be bringing cupcakes with sprinkles if her mother felt good enough to make them or, if she didn't, either Hostess Twinkies or Hostess Sno Balls. Eugene Bowen was bringing potato chips on account of his father was a driver for State Line. "Aw, crap," Lonny said. "*I* was gonna bring potato chips. Okay, I'll bring napkins then."

Bridget Mann: Scottish shortbread cookies.

Monte Montoya: sopaipilla cheesecake pie.

Jackie Burnham: plum pudding.

Edgy Chang: Chinese almond cookies.

Me: pizelles. (The Christmas before, Pop had given Ma a bottle of perfume, a bottle of anisette from Italy, and a pizelle iron.)

Rosalie: Polish poppyseed roll, rum babka with marzipan Christmas decorations, and *chrusciki.* "Otherwise known as angel wings," Rosalie added. "And I'll have my mother put extra powdered sugar on them. They're *so* good."

"How about you, Zhenya?" Madame said. "Will your mother be able to make something?"

"Een our house, my fodder eese cooker," she said. "He mek for party samouk vid pruns."

"Did you say prunes, Zhenya?" Madame said.

"Ya, ya. He mek dat end he mek strudel vid meelk curds end raisins."

Prunes and raisins? Milk curds? Well, it could have been worse, I figured. At least she wasn't bringing that stinky herring she ate at lunchtime.

"*Merveilleux!*" Madame said, clapping her hands together. "Our food table will be worthy of *l'Organisation des Nations Unies!* And I myself shall add two desserts *québecoise* to our *fête internationale.*" She wrote what she was making on the board—*tartelettes au sucre* and *bûche de Noël au chocolat*—then turned back toward us, beaming. "Sounds good. *Oui?*"

We said it in unison. "*Oui,* Madame."

7

Noël

By the Thursday before "the big shew," things were falling nicely into place. Ernie Overturf and his dad arrived at school in their pickup truck and a bunch of us boys helped them unload the plywood animals they'd made: stand-up cows, sheep, a donkey, identical triplet camels. Mr. Overturf and Mr. Dombrowski, our janitor, carried the biggest and heaviest prop: the front of the stable where Jesus was going to get born in the big finale. (There was nothing in back; just these wooden braces that held it up. Madame said it was a "façade," which was one of the many, many English words that everyone had the French to thank for.)

Madame had cast the three MaryAnns as angels in the final nativity scene and Franz Duzio as the only boy angel, Gabriel, in the Annunciation *tableau*. MaryAnn V.'s mother had gone to Careen's Costumes and rented four curly blond wigs, four sets of wings, and these really cool halos that you put batteries in and they lit up. Madame told the MaryAnns to wear floor-length nightgowns—white ones. Franz Duzio wanted to know what *he* was supposed to wear, and Madame said a white night*shirt* if he had one, and Franz said he didn't—that he just slept in his underpants, and when he said that, some of the girls covered their mouths with their hands. Well, then, Madame said, maybe his mother or sister had a nightgown that he might borrow. Glaring at the rest of us, Franz scanned the room, trying to locate who had just laughed. (Me.)

Mrs. Kubiak had dropped off, along with the

twins, a half dozen bales of hay, the corn crib that would be Jesus's manger, and enough burlap bags from Thompson's Feed & Grain to clothe all nine shepherdesses and shepherds. And the Kubiaks' older brother, who went to trade school instead of regular high school, had made us this big silver star of Bethlehem that had sockets that you could put Christmas bulbs in. We were using that for the shepherds' *tableau*, the Wise Men's *tableau*, and the nativity *tableau*. And this was cool: Ronald and Roland's brother had even rigged up this special pulley-and-rope thing that you could raise and lower the star with.

There was a kind of contest between Bridget Mann and Margaret Elizabeth McCormick about which one's baby doll was going to get picked to be Jesus. Madame Frechette said that, since Bridget's doll didn't look as "well-used" as Margaret Elizabeth's, and since it still had both of its glass eyes, that was the one she was picking, but that Margaret Elizabeth's doll could be the understudy. When Margaret Elizabeth heard the news, she started crying, so

Madame took her out in the hallway for a talk, and while they were gone, Zhenya asked, out loud to no one in particular, "What det is? Onderstoody?"

Several of us shrugged, but from across the room, Franz Duzio said, "Means the one-eyed doll's gonna sit the bench and never get in the game."

"Gemm?" Zhenya said. "Vut gemme you means?"

"Bezbull," Franz said, imitating her.

Zhenya laughed at that. "Franz, you big cuckoo head," she said. "You no play bezbull vit bebby dull."

Rosalie told them they'd both better shut up. "Because the rule is, whenever Madame is out of the room, we're supposed to carry on in silence. *Remember?*"

"Oh, ya ya," Zhenya retorted. "I forgetted det. Tenk you for remembering me about it, cheeky bum-bum geuhl." She looked over at me and winked.

Margaret Elizabeth was dry eyed when her and Madame came back in the room, but now she was pouting. I overheard her telling Kitty Callahan that understudies were stupid and she was just bringing her doll home.

On Friday, we all had to bring in our costumes and try them on in the boys' and girls' rooms after lunch and then come out and show Madame so she could approve them. When Madame saw Lonny in the costume Simone had put together for him, I watched her eyes move from Anna Ianuzzi's blue garter stretched over his dish-toweled head down to where my bathrobe ended and Lonny's bare legs began. Madame asked if, *peut-être*, he had a robe that dropped a little further down. "This is Felix's bathrobe," he said. "I ain't got one."

"Do you think your mother might be able to purchase you one that's a better fit?" When Lonny shook his head, Madame nodded and told him, very well then, she guessed his costume would be okay.

Pauline Papelbon's Mary costume got okayed, too, which kinda surprised me. Pauline told Madame that her neighbors, the Madraswallas, were Indians—from India, not cowboys-and-Indians Indians—and so she'd borrowed this sari thing that showed some of her bloopy stomach in the middle between the top part and the bottom part, plus this sorta see-through veil. I thought Pauline looked not so much like the Blessed Virgin as she did that lady in my *1001 Arabian Nights* book—the one that had to keep telling the king stories so he wouldn't croak her. But I guess Madame didn't think that.

When I came out in my costume, everyone was saying all this wiseguy stuff like what was it like meeting George Washington, and how was the Boston Tea Party? And I was like ha, ha, ha, that was so funny I forgot to laugh. (Pop says that, when someone's teasing you, don't give them the satisfaction of letting them know it's bugging you.) But when Arthur Coté told me I had knock knees, I kinda forgot Pop's advice and jabbed him with one of my chopstick drumsticks—not *that* hard, but hard enough to leave this little red mark that kinda looked like a bullet hole. Arthur didn't squeal on me, though. I bet if I'd poked Rosalie like that, she probably would've skipped Mother Filomina and gone right to Pope Paul to see if he'd excommunication me.

All's the shepherds and shepherdesses had to do for their costumes was cut holes in the top of their burlap feed bags, slip them over their heads, and tie a rope around their waist. But from the looks of it, Zhenya had gone a little crazy with the scissors when she was cutting *her* head hole. You couldn't see her bazoom-booms or anything, but if she'd cut away a few more inches, you maybe could've. Scrawny Geraldine and Zhenya were standing next to each other in the inspection line, and it reminded me of down at the lunch counter—looking first at Annette when she was in *Mickey Mouse Club* and then at the poster of her from *Beach Blanket Bingo*—the one I French-kissed and had to have that talk with Monsignor about. When Zhenya asked Madame if, during the shepherds' scene, she could wear her Carnaby Street cap, too, Madame put her hand over her heart and went, "*Non, non, non!*"

"H'okay, boss lady," Zhenya said, patting Madame's arm and smiling. "I nut wear het. H'everytink eese groovy, ya ya?"

Rosalie's costumes were the fanciest—*both* of

them. For her Wise Man outfit, her parents had paid some seamstress to make her this long red velvet cape with fake white fur trim. Plus, after Turdski and her mother went to Careen's Costumes and didn't find anything they thought was good enough, they drove to this other costume place all the way down in *New York City!* Down there, they rented this fancy-looking crown with big fake jewels that looked real. Plus, they bought Rosalie a fake beard and a tube of this stuff called spirit gum that *real actors* use to stick beards and things on their face with. As the narrator of her play, Rosalie was wearing one of her mother's old evening gowns and these long, dangly earrings, and *another* crown that Rosalie kept telling everyone was "an exact replica of Miss America's crown." Mother Filomina had okayed her wearing makeup, too— lipstick *and* eyeshadow—but only for her play, and then she'd have to go to the girls' room and take it right off before she came out as Caspar the Wise Man. Plus, Mother said, none of the *other* fifth grade girls had better get any ideas about wearing makeup for the *tableaux*. This was just a one-time special privilege because Rosalie'd written her stupid play.

Like Rosalie, Marion Pemberton had two parts, Saint Martin de Porres and the black Wise Man, but he was wearing his same costume for both, on account of, even though Rosalie didn't want him to, Madame Frechette said he could. Marion's mother had sewn his costume out of an old shiny silver sheet, and she made him a turban out of a pillowcase that went with the sheet, and I thought he looked pretty cool.

I thought the three MaryAnns looked good, too, in their white nightgowns and angel wings and light-up halos. But one angel didn't look so hot: Franz Duzio. With his bushy black eyebrows, his curly blond wig, and this lady's nightgown he had to borrow "from my fat aunt," Franz looked not so much like the Angel Gabriel as he did some psycho combination of Cupid and Shirley Temple. When he first came out of the boys' room in his get-up, a bunch of us started giggling. We couldn't help it. But Franz said whoever *kept* laughing was gonna get beaten to a bloody pulp as soon as we got off school property. So after that, nobody laughed. Franz was the second oldest and toughest boy in our class after Lonny, and in a fight he might even be able to take Lonny, I'm not sure. Not that they were *gonna* fight or anything. Franz and Lonny got along pretty good. When they arm-wrestled during indoor recess, sometimes Lonny won and sometimes Franz did, but they always shook hands afterwards like gentlemen.

Saturday afternoon was dress rehearsal for every single kid who was in the Christmas program. Attendance was mandatory, Sister Fabian said over the P.A. the day before, which meant you *had* to be there unless you or one of your parents were croaking or something. Or maybe one of your grandparents.

The first and second graders were lucky stiffs.

Even though they were going on second to *last* in the program the next day, they got to practice *first* because Sister Fabian said they'd get ants in their pants if they had to wait around. They were singing the only song in the whole show that wasn't holy. This is what they were doing: first Father Hanrahan comes out on the stage carrying this fake Christmas tree. Then he goes to the audience, "Hey, do you folks hear what I hear?" And backstage, there's these jingle bells that the audience can hear but not see yet. Then one of the stage hands—Ernie Overturf's older brother, Richard, who's in eighth grade but doesn't play a musical instrument—starts a record backstage and holds a microphone up to the speaker. And all the first and second graders come out holding hands, and they start circling the tree and singing "Rockin' Around the Christmas Tree" along with Brenda Lee (not the real her, just the record). Plus, every first and second grader's wearing reindeer antlers and they got jingle bells tied to their shoelaces—which was where the jingle bell sounds were coming from when Father asked, "Hey, do you hear what I hear?" See, while they're still backstage, all the little kids shake their feet to make their jingle bells jingle.

After the little kids got to leave dress rehearsal, the eighth grade orchestra, seventh grade choir, sixth grade chorus, and fourth grade glee club all got to practice *their* musical numbers with Mrs. Button, the music teacher. (Mrs. Button and Madame were our school's only lay teachers, which all that means is they're not nuns.) The music sounded okay, except the eighth grade orchestra kinda stunk a little, especially the screechy violins. Anyways, us *tableaux* kids had to just hang around and wait while all the musicians rehearsed, and it was *so boring*. Then? When the sixth grade chorus was practicing that "We Three Kings" song, Lonny and me started singing the funny version:

We three kings of Orient are
Tried to smoke a rubber cigar . . .

We had to shut up, though, because Sister Fabian gave us a dirty look and said something about being sacrilegious. And right after that? Pauline Papelbon walked by Lonny and Franz and me, eating Fritos in her Mary costume with her stomach kinda stickin' out, and Franz went to Lonny that, since Lonny was Joseph and Pauline was Mary, he sure must be glad that the baby was God's son, not *his*, because Pauline was probably the *last* girl Lonny would wanna do you-know-what with.

"You better watch it," I warned Franz. "That's *real* sacrilegious." But Franz ignored me and started making pig snorts in Pauline's direction, which Lonny *kinda* laughed at a little, but then he stopped. I didn't laugh at all because it was pretty mean. Plus, Pauline never really bothered anybody. And if her mother had to go to the state hospital last year, which everyone knew about, that wasn't *her* fault. To tell you the truth, I was a little bit glad she got picked to be Mary, on account of Pauline hardly ever got picked for anything, and the only other girl I ever seen sit with her in the lunch room was her seventh grade sister, Claudette, who, come to think of it, was kind of a chowhound, too. But anyways, like I said, I didn't think dress rehearsal was all that fair, because even though *we* had to wait around for all the musicians to get done, after they finished, they got to leave instead of hanging around waiting for *us*.

This was the way Madame said it was gonna go. For each *tableau* (except the last one), there would be two songs: one *before* the curtain opened and one *after* it did. "So for the Annunciation, *par exemple*, the seventh graders will sing 'Angels We Have Heard on High.' Then the curtain will open to reveal the Angel Gabriel telling the Virgin the news that she is with child. And as that scene is revealed to the audience, the orchestra plays and the soloist sings the 'Ave Maria.' *Vous comprenez?*" We all said yeah. This kid Happy Rocketto? Who was on my last year's Little League team? His sister's the soloist, and she has this kind of opera voice. When Zhenya heard her during rehearsal, she said, "Wow-ee, I luff opera. That geuhl sing bootyful, ya Fillix?" and I said yeah, but what I was really thinking was yuck, get me some earplugs.

After the Annunciation would come the shepherds' scene, Madame said, then Rosalie's play, and then the Magi scene. (Which meant Rosalie had to change real fast from her narrator gown into her king costume *and* get all of her narrator eyeshadow and lipstick off.) "After the Kindergarteners' song and 'Away in a Manger,' we shall have the big finale with the Christ child and all who have come to adore Him," Madame said. Which was the *tableau* I was in—me and our whole class except for the Kubiak brothers who were stagehands, and so they got to just set up and take down things like the hay bales and plywood animals and not have to wear a costume and go out on stage and act paralyzed and practically not even breathe until the curtain closed. The Kubiaks were also in charge of keeping the lambs quiet until the last *tableau*—the real lambs, not the plywood ones. Oh, and Mr. Dombrowski, our janitor, he was kinda like a stagehand, too, I guess, because he was in charge of working the rope that was gonna raise and lower the star of Bethlehem. It was pretty cool, that pulley thing, and some of us boys wanted to try raising and lowering it, but Madame said no, not even the Kubiak twins could do it, even though it was their own brother who made it. Only Mr. Dombrowski could.

Near the end of dress rehearsal, I got yelled at by Madame Frechette. I deserved it, kind of. In the middle of rehearsing kids, Madame had taken off her beret and left it on a chair backstage. And me and Oscar Landry and Monte Montoya started playing frisbee with it, and she caught us. She yelled at all three of us, but mostly at me because when she asked whose idea it was, Oscar and Monte both pointed at me. We all said we were sorry and Madame nodded, stuck her beret back on, and didn't give us detention.

At the end of dress rehearsal, Madame reminded us that the Christmas program started promptly at 2:00 P.M. the next afternoon, but that everyone should get dropped off no later than 1:00 P.M. so we could get into our costumes and wait on the stair landing until our *tableau* came up and it was time for us to tip-toe down the back stairs, get into our places on stage, and freeze. Then she had us all sit on the stage floor, and she started walking back and forth in front of us with her hands on her hips, and giving us a speech. "You must remember, *mes élèves*, that as the singers and players will be celebrating *la nativité* with their music, you are the ones who will *embody* the Christmas story!" When she said the word "embody," she closed her eyes and put her hands up in the air. We all kind of looked at each other funny and waited, cause it looked like she was in a trance or something.

After Madame opened her eyes again, she said, "Should your nose itch while the curtain remains open, you must resist the urge to scratch it. Should you wish to gaze out upon the audience to see if you can spot your family, you must forbid yourself to do so." She adjusted her beret, took one hand off of one hip, and left the other one on her other hip. "Any questions?"

Susan Ekizian raised her hand. "What if we hafta sneeze?"

"Then you must suppress it, *mademoiselle*."

"How?" someone else asked.

Madame shrugged. "However you are able. Perhaps by digging your fingernails into your leg or forcing yourself to think about something else—something sad, perhaps, or something joyous. And if, in your nervousness, the urge to laugh comes over you, then you must bite your lip hard, drawing a drop or two of blood if you have to, but you must not, under any circumstances, break the illusion that you are a living, three-dimensional painting as breathtaking and beautiful as any in the Louvre." Madame had told us a million times about the time she visited the Louvre. (Which is in Paris, France. See, England owns Canada, but if you live in Québec, you like France better.)

When we finally got out of dress rehearsal, both

Simone and Frances were waiting for me in our station wagon. It was strange to see Frances and not Simone behind the wheel. Fran had gotten her learner's permit the week before, but Ma and Pop were too busy to give her driving lessons, so Simone was doing it. I got in the backseat without saying anything. And I *kept* not saying anything, too, on the way home until finally Simone looked back at me and said, "How come *you're* so quiet today, Felix?"

"I'm just tired," I said.

"Yeah, standing still on a stage is really exhausting, huh?" Frances said. And I went "Shut up," and Fran said why didn't *I* shut up, and Simone told her to stop bickering and concentrate on the road.

The real reason I was being so quiet was because I was worried. What if, just as the curtain opened and they started singing "The Little Drummer Boy," I got diarrhea like Ma at the Bake-Off? I wasn't going to tell my sisters that, though, because Frances would probably lose control of the car from laughing so hard and get us into a crack-up. In my opinion,

I didn't think Simone should be teaching Frances how to drive because Simone wasn't that hot a driver herself. Whenever she had to parallel park, she either ended up on the curb or else three feet away from it.

Most Saturday nights I got to stay up and watch *Gunsmoke*, but that night Ma made me go to bed at 9:30 because the next day was gonna be such a big day for me. Here's who was coming to the *tableaux* to see me: Ma, Simone, Frances, and my Nonna Napolitano, if her corns weren't bothering her too bad. Pop said he was gonna *try* to come, but he couldn't make any promises. On account of, with everyone traveling for the holiday, the bus station was gonna be real, real busy and so the manager, Mr. Popinchalk, told Pop he wanted him to keep the lunch counter open all day and not close early like we usually did on Sundays. And Chino was still getting over the flu, so he was "iffy," Pop said. If Chino couldn't work, then

Pop definitely wouldn't be able to come. "But I'll do my best to get there, kiddo," he promised me.

At first, I couldn't get to sleep because I was too excited. Then I started worrying again about sneezing, or having to laugh, or getting the runs. Then, finally, I started getting tired. I closed my eyes and was just about falling asleep when my stupid imagination made me see it again: Joseph Cotten's chopped-off head bouncing bumpity bump bump bump down those stairs. . . .

When Ma finally let me get up and have warm milk and Saltines, the 11:00 o'clock news was already on. So, really, I coulda watched *Gunsmoke* because I was awake all that time anyway. And it was way after midnight when I finally went into Ma and Pop's bedroom, and woke up Ma, and whispered, "I'm *still* not sleeping." And Pop moaned and went, "Oh, brother. Here we go again." But he was the one who said I could go get my sleeping bag and then come back and camp out on the floor at the foot of their bed.

And after I did that, I fell asleep in about two seconds.

* * *

ST. ALOYSIUS GONZAGA

PAROCHIAL SCHOOL

Christmas Program

Sunday December 20, 1964

WELCOMING REMARKS:

Mother M. Filomina, Principal

OPENING BENEDICTION:

Monsignor Angus P. Muldoon, Pastor

PLEDGE OF ALLEGIANCE:

Kevin Wojcik, Grade 8 Class President

MASTER OF CEREMONIES:

Rev. Gerald "Jerry" Hanrahan, Pastoral Vicar

I.

"Angels We Have Heard on High"
Grade 7 Choir

Tableau # 1: The Annunciation
Students of Grade 5

"Ave Maria" Grade 8 Orchestra
w/ Margaret Rocketto, soloist

II.

"While Shepherds Watched Their Flocks"
Grade 6 Chorus

Tableau # 2: Shepherds in Their Fields
Students of Grade 5

"It Came Upon a Midnight Clear"
Grade 6 Chorus

III.

A DRAMATIC INTERLUDE:
"JESUS IS THE REASON FOR THE SEASON"

Saint Aloysius Gonzaga: Ernest Overturf
(Grade 5)

Saint Martin de Porres: Marion Pemberton
(Grade 5)

Saint Teresa Lisieux: Geraldine Balchunas
(Grade 5)

Written, narrated, & produced by
Rosalie Elaine Twerski (Grade 5)

IV.

"It Came Upon a Midnight Clear"
Grade 7 Choir

Tableau # 3: The Wise Men's Journey

Students of Grade 5

"We Three Kings of Orient Are"

Grade 8 Orchestra w. Grade 6 Chorus

V.

"Rockin' Around the Christmas Tree"

Grades 1 and 2 w/ Father "Jerry"

VI.

"Away in a Manger" Grade 4 Glee Club

Tableau # 4: The Nativity

Students of Grade 5

"The Little Drummer Boy"

Grade 7 Choir

"Joy to the World" Grade 7 Choir &
Grade 6 Chorus

Closing Remarks:
Father "Jerry"

"God Bless America"
Entire Company & Audience

Families are invited back to their sons' and daughters' classrooms for refreshments after the program. Parents who bring desserts are reminded to take home their trays before they leave the building as food attracts insects. Thanks to everyone!

A Happy and HOLY Christmas to All!
THIS PROGRAM COURTESY OF TWERSKI IMPRESSIONS, 176 HOLLYHOCK HILL, THREE RIVERS, CONNECTICUT. AT TWERSKI IMPRESSIONS, WE'RE ON THE HILL BUT ON THE LEVEL.

STOP IN & SEE US, NEIGHBORS, FOR ALL YOUR PRINTING NEEDS!!!

Pauline Papelbon's mother *was* too sick to make those cupcakes, and so Pauline, instead, brought in a whole big bag of Hostess Sno Balls for her refreshment. And I guess if she'd have brought them up to our classroom like Madame had told us to, instead of keeping them with her on the stair landing, maybe things would have turned out different. Or maybe they wouldn't have. Who knows?

The first thing that went wrong—not too wrong, just kind of—was that Monsignor Muldoon might have been a little bit drunk. When he walked past us on the stair landing on his way to give his benediction, instead of smelling like Butter Rum Life Savers, he smelled a little like Mush Moriarty. Monsignor slipped a little on the stairs when he started down there for his opening benediction, but then he caught himself. And when he went out on the stage? Frances said he was kinda teeter-tottering a little and holding on to the microphone stand to steady himself. (The rest of us *tableaux* kids all had to wait up on the stair landing and couldn't see anything; we could only hear things.) Ma said maybe Monsignor was just having a little trouble with his balance, and that "that's the way false rumors get started, young lady." But when I mentioned that I'd smelled him and he kind of smelled like Mush, Ma said, "Well, whether he was or wasn't tipsy, it's certainly none of *our* business."

Then the eighth grade president, that Kevin kid, got stage fright while he was leading the Pledge of Allegiance. He must have, I figured, because he was sorta laughing in the middle of saying it, and there's nothing really funny about the Pledge of Allegiance, except when Zhenya says it: *I plidge leejinks to flig h'uv United Stets h'uv H'Ametekka.* Ma said later that she didn't think anyone even noticed the class president was laughing, and Frances said, "Oh, yes they did!"

During the first *tableau*, Happy Rocketto's sister's voice cracked a little during "Ave Maria." Twice.

And Frances and Simone both said later on that Franz Duzio looked like he was picking his nose a little in the middle of his scene. "And eating it!" Frances added. Simone said no he wasn't, but Fran said yes he was, she'd swear on a stack of Bibles.

Simone said she thought Pauline Papelbon did good—that she didn't hardly move her arms at all, even though she had to hold them up in the air in this position like *Oh, my gosh! Really?* because Gabriel is telling her she's gonna get pregnant with God's baby. Then Frances said, after Simone said that Pauline did a good job, "Yeah, but how come she was wearing a costume that made her look like Scheherazade?" (Which was the same lady *I* thought her costume made her look like—the one from *1001 Arabian Nights*.) And when Fran said that, Ma said, "Frances Ann Funicello, do you have to criticize *every*one and *every*thing?" And Frances went, no, she didn't have to, she just *wanted* to. So Ma went, "I suppose if *you* were in charge, everything would be perfect. Right?" and Fran went, "Yeah, probably."

The shepherds' *tableau* went pretty okay, I guess, except in the middle of the sixth graders singing "It Came Upon a Midnight Clear," we all heard this noise like *bang*. And before that, I heard this guy from the audience yell, "Yoo hoo, Evgeniya! Ooo-wee! Nice job, leetle geuhl!" and I was pretty sure who *that* was. At least he didn't get up on stage and give her one of those little kicks in her rear end the way he did when he walked her to school. After all the shepherds came back upstairs, Arthur told me what that bang was: one of the plywood sheeps that Mr. Overturf had made fell over. I said, "Did someone bump into it or something?" and Arthur got all red and mad and he said, "Well, *I* didn't! What are you accusing *me* for?" So I thought that maybe he did.

Rosalie's play? At the beginning, you could hear people in the audience oohing and ahhing when she walked out on stage in her fancy gown and crown and up on the stair landing, Franz started singing, *There she is, Miss America,* and everyone laughed a little, even some of the girls. At dress rehearsal, Ernie Overturf had complained to me that whenever Turdski made them practice their parts, she was always acting bossy and yelling at them to speak louder. And boy, when him and Marion and Geraldine came on, they sure *were* loud. It sounded like they were all yelling at each other!

Geraldine messed up one of her Saint Teresa lines. Instead of saying, "If you subtract 1873 from 1897, you get 24, which was very young for me to die," she said, "If you subtract *1897* from *1873.*" And when she said, "You get 24," some wiseguy high school kid yelled out from the audience, "No you don't. You get *negative* 24. That's *really* young!" And you could hear some people laughing and other people *not* laughing.

Then when Geraldine said to Marion, "Why are you so sad, Saint Martin de Porres? Is it because prejudiced people are so mean to colored people?" instead of Marion saying what Rosalie had written for him to say, he said, "They are, are they? Well, wait'll the NAACP hears about *this!*" And then you could hear *everyone* out there laughing, not just some people. Everyone, that is, except Rosalie. Frances and Simone both said she looked like she was gonna bop Marion one. I guess the rest of the play went okay. At least I didn't hear about anything else that went wrong. Oh, yeah—wait a minute. Yes, I did. Some kid threw a bottle cap at Rosalie and it hit her on the forehead. Sister Godberta saw who it was: this kid Lenny Thomas who graduated from St. Aloysius the year before. He got kicked out—escorted by Sister Lucinda on one side and Sister Agnes on the other, and behind them, this bald guy who passes the basket at Mass and looks like Uncle Fester on *The Addams Family*.

When the play got over and the curtain closed, Rosalie was half-crying and half-screaming at Marion that he wrecked her whole play, but she was also having to hurry, because she had to get into her Wise Man clothes and get her makeup off, plus stick her fake beard on with that spirit gum stuff, and all's the time she had to do it in was the time it took for the seventh grade choir to sing, "It Came Upon a Midnight Clear." It wasn't *that* bad, though, because Madame gave Mrs. Twerski permission to come backstage and help her change. Plus, the seventh graders were singing *all* the verses of "It Came Upon a Midnight Clear," not just the first couple, on account of Rosalie having to change.

Here's why things might have been way different if Pauline hadn't kept her Hostess Sno Balls with her on the stair landing. I seen her eating at least one package of Sno Balls before The Annunciation even, and then a bunch of other kids in our class said they saw her eating at least four more Sno Balls during the shepherds' and Wise Men's scenes and Rosalie's play. No one really knew how many she ate, but afterwards when I looked inside her bag, it looked to me like there was more empty cellophane than there was unopened packages.

Anyways, *downstairs?* Right at the part where Father Jerry was bringing out the fake Christmas tree and going to the audience, "Do you folks hear what I hear?" *Up*stairs, Pauline started crying and holding her stomach and saying how she didn't feel good. So Madame went over to her and said what's the matter, and Pauline said she was having the worst stomach-ache of her whole life. Madame told her to put her head down between her legs and take deep breaths. And when Pauline did that, she started crying louder and saying that made her feel even worse and she was maybe gonna have to puke. And so Madame looked around and spotted Rosalie's mother standing there. And she said, "Mrs. Twerski, take Pauline to the girls' room, *s'il vous plait*." And Mrs. Twerski started saying something about how maybe Madame should be the one to—and Madame cut her off and said, in this kind of yelly voice, *"Maintenant, Madame!"* Which in French means like, "Now! Step on it, lady!" And so Mrs. Twerski took hold of a little bit of Pauline's veil with her fingernails and they started toward the girls' room. But halfway there, Pauline stopped and she did puke, and some of it got on Mrs. Twerski, who used a swear word right in front of all us kids. And I thought, wow, between Danny Baldino on the bus on the way to Hartford and now poor Pauline, I sure had seen a lot of kids puking in just one month.

(And I wasn't even counting that trick that Lonny played on me Halloween night, cause that was just fake puke, not real puke.)

Madame started looking at us all with these kinda crazy eyes. Then she snatched Bridget's baby doll away from her and, holding it in one hand, pointed at Zhenya with the other. "*Mademoiselle*, you're Mary!" she said.

Zhenya shrugged. "How I be hair? No custoom h'except shepairdess."

Madame's crazy eyes found Franz. "Change costumes with Zhenya," she ordered him. Franz's eyes kinda bugged out and he told her he couldn't—that all's he had on underneath his fat aunt's nightgown was his underwear. But Zhenya had already slipped her feed sack over her head and was standing there in *her* underwear—pink polka dot underpants on the bottom and just this white bra on top! "Come on, beeg boyzy," she said to Franz. "Ticher wants h'us to sweetch, we sweetch." And so they did. (And for the rest of that school year and into the next, kids talked about seeing the two of them standing there for a few seconds with almost no clothes on.) But while Zhenya was getting into Franz's nightgown and and he was getting into her burlap sack, I looked over at Lonny and thought to myself, *uh oh*. Because in just a few more minutes, while he was wearing my too-short-for-him bathrobe, Lonny was going to have to walk out on the stage and be Joseph, and there it was again, triggered, no doubt, by the sight of his "geuhlfriend" in just her underwear: what Zhenya had once referred to as "feeshing pole" in Lonny's "paints." Panic-stricken, Lonny saw that I saw what was going on down there, and, hunchbacked, he sidestepped over to me and whispered, "I can't go out there like this! What the crap should I do?"

At first I couldn't think of anything, but then I did. "You know that movie we saw? *Hush . . . Hush, Sweet Charlotte?*"

"Yeah?"

"Remember the part where that guy got his head chopped off by the meat cleaver?"

"Yeah? What about it?"

"Pretend someone's swinging that meat cleaver at you. Except instead of your head, it's about to come down right on your—" Lonny winced and doubled over even further. And by the time he stood up straight again, I saw that my idea had begun to work. Lonny said I was a genius.

Madame handed Bridget's baby doll to Zhenya. That was when the big fight started. Because Rosalie, who was still wearing her Wise Man costume, went kinda cuckoo and started *screaming* at Madame. "It's not fair! I work harder than anyone in this whole class and you never appreciate it! And why *her* of all people? She's an atheist, and a Communist, and she's only been in our class since November! And you're just a stupid substitute so I don't care what you say! *I'm Mary!*" And with that, Turdski made a grab for Baby Jesus.

But Zhenya, who'd told me she was "Russian Ortudox" not "no beleef in Gud," was not about to relinquish the Christ Child to her chief critic. She held fast to the doll's feet as Rosalie pulled it by its head. The rest of us, Madame included, stood there stunned. Something had to give, I figured, and then something did.

As the doll's head ripped away from its torso, Rosalie fell backward and let go. In horror, I watched the head bounce bumpity bump bump down the backstage stairs. Now, like Lonny a few minutes earlier, it was me who was wincing and doubling over. Joseph Cotten, Jesus: I would probably *never, ever,* get to sleep again. And when I finally was able to look up at something other than the floor, I found myself looking into the wild eyes of Madame Frechette.

"Monsieur Dondi!" she said. "Remove your hat, *chemise,* and *pantalons.*"

I began to shake. "My what?"

"Your shirt! Your pants! *Dépêchez-vous!* There is very little time!"

"I can't," I said. "I'm the little drummer boy!"

She shook her head furiously. "No more! Now you have a much more important part. You are our Baby Jesus! Hurry!"

Now I was shaking *my* head furiously. "I can't! I'm too big!" A stupid argument, given the fact that I was the smallest kid in our class, boys *and* girls.

"The show must go on," Madame said. And then, using the same tone of voice she had used on Mrs. Twerski, *"Maintenant, Monsieur!"*

I told Madame that, okay, I would remove my *chemise* for the sake of our *tableau*, but I wasn't taking off my *pantalons* for anything. Madame nodded in agreement, so I agreed to be Jesus.

Downstairs, behind the curtain, the Kubiaks rushed about, setting up the props for the big nativity finale, then ran to retrieve the live lambs they'd sequestered in a coop upstairs in our classroom. Out front, jingle bells were jingling. Accompanied by Brenda Lee's vocal—*You will get a sentimental feeling when you hear/Voices singing "Let's be jolly, deck the halls with boughs of ha-olly"*—Madame positioned all of her players except Lonny, Zhenya, and me, her 66 percent recast Holy Family. Yanking the silver turban from Marion Pemberton's head, she ripped the pillowcase apart with almost superhuman strength, transformed it into a veil for Zhenya, and ordered her to kneel beside the manger. "And you, *monsieur*, kneel in the crib!" she ordered me. When I did so, she told Franz to hand her his blond Shirley Temple wig. Grabbing it from him, she stretched the wig over my skull. Then, in a sort of frenzy, she pulled apart one of the hay bales and stuffed straw around everything below my chest. "The doll!" she called over to Bridget, the way Dr. Kildare called for an instrument in the middle of an operation. Bridget handed Madame her headless baby doll, and Madame stuck it into the end of the corn crib opposite my head, then fussed some more with handfuls of straw. When she stepped away, Baby Jesus had my head and shoulders and, sticking out the other end, infant-sized rubber feet.

On the other side of the curtain, "Rockin' Around the Christmas Tree" was winding down and, one by one, the first and second graders began jingling off the stage to the sound of applause and cheering. In the nick of time, the Kubiaks returned with the live lambs. Roland handed his to Eugene and Ronald placed his in Jackie Burnham's waiting arms. "Aww," everyone kept saying. "They're so cute!"

"Shhh!" Madame said. *"Ecoutez!"* By now, her red beret had slid back so far on her head that I wondered how it was staying on. The sixth graders were halfway through their second verse of "Away in a Manger" when I looked over at Rosalie, who was tugging on her fake beard and ripping it away in clumps. She'd managed to yank off most of it, but not the part still stuck to her chin. Then she reached around and pulled the back end of her velvet Wise Man cape over her head and hurried over to my manger. Kneeling beside Zhenya, she reached over and gave her a two-handed shove. Out front, the sixth graders were down to, *"And stay by my cradle till morning is nigh,"* and the curtain, in another ten seconds or so, would part.

Zhenya shoved back. Rosalie retaliated with a harder shove.

My eyes found Madame, standing in the wings. One of our vocab words the week before was "transfixed" and that's what Madame was: as trans-fixed as someone in a *tableau vivant* as she watched the two combatting Marys.

Zhenya's next shove knocked Rosalie back onto the floor. Trying to right herself, she reached out and accidentally grabbed Zhenya by her bazoom-booms. I was staring in shock—we all were—when Lonny called "Felix!"

He'd been staring, too, I guess, and when he'd seen where Rosalie's hands had landed, he'd begun having his problem again. As the curtain began to part, I lifted an imaginary meat cleaver over my head and brought it down with a vicious *whack!* To my relief, and more important, to Lonny's, he doubled over once more.

At first, the audience was stunned to silence as it stared upon what, I'm guessing, was the most bizarre nativity they'd ever seen. For there before them, be-low the electrified Star of Bethlehem, was a Baby Jesus with shrunken feet, a bent-at-the-waist Joseph, and not one but two Marys, one of whom seemed to be wearing a goatee.

The seventh graders began singing "The Little Drummer Boy," but, of course, the little drummer boy was a no-show, his shelf-papered hat box and chopsticks abandoned backstage. The crowd started mumbling and murmuring. The murmuring turned steadily into snickering and, by the choir's closing *pa-rumpa-pum-pums*, many audience members were ... what's that word? Guffawing.

By the time "Joy to the World" began, the laughter had begun to die down—until, that is, Ernie Overturf's brother Richard accidentally bumped into Mr. Dombrowski, who, startled, let go of his rope for a second or two, then grabbed onto it again, then let go for a second time, then made another grab— the effect of which, on stage, was that the Star of Bethlehem seemed to keep changing its mind about whether it wanted to be a shooting star or one that remained high in the heavens. And when I looked over in the wings again? Madame wasn't transfixed anymore. Now she was doing something really weird: drinking perfume from one of those two bottles I'd seen in her purse that day when I had to go up and get her sunglasses. Not her lily-of-the-valley perfume but the other one: cognac.

After "Joy to the World" ended and the curtain closed again, Father Jerry began his closing remarks to the audience. "Well, I'm sure every one of you will agree that this has been just about the most memorable Christmas program in the entire United States of America—or maybe I should say, the United States of *Hysteria*."

Everyone laughed at that.

"But the kids and their teachers have all worked very hard on today's event, so let's first of all give a hand to Mrs. Lillian Button and her wonderful singers and players, to whom we say, "If music be the gift of life, play on!" Out front, there was lots of cheering for the musicians. I was glad Father Jerry wasn't saying anything about us, because I didn't want to get booed at.

But then Father Jerry said, "And, of course, there's our actors to thank as well. Ladies and gentlemen, this afternoon you've seen the world premiere of "Jesus Is the Reason for the Season" by Saint Aloysius Gonzaga's very own fifth-grade playwright, Rosalie Twerski, and you've also witnessed on this historic afternoon Saint Aloysius G's first-ever *tableaux vivants,* which I sure hope will now become an annual tradition at this great school. And who knows, maybe by next year we may even have those couple of little kinks worked out for you." That made people laugh. "So why don't we get the curtain open again and have our players and their director *extraordinaire,* Mrs. Marguerite Frechette, step forward and take a bow. ("Oh my god," Simone noted later. "The audience gave you guys a standing ovation." When I asked what that was, Ma was the one who answered. "It means everyone liked you so much, they got up off their *culos* to cheer for you.")

When the others stepped to the front of the stage to take their bow, I was too embarrassed to get up, so I stayed put in my corn crib. But when Lonny looked back and saw me, he had him and Ronnie Kubiak carry the manger up to the front, too. And when they did that, everyone cheered kinda loud, and so I waved at them and that made them cheer even louder. And while I was looking out at the audience, I found Ma, Simone, and Frances. They were in the fourth row, right in the middle. Nonna wasn't with them, though, so I guess her corns were bothering her. I kept looking for Pop, but he wasn't there, so I figured Chino musta still been sick. And then? I *did* see Pop. He was way over on the side, three quarters of the way back, between this old lady who must have been somebody's grandma and this other, younger lady with big giant hair and a kerchief. And when I waved, Pop waved back, and so did the kerchief lady next to him and I was like, I wasn't waving to *you*, Mrs. Big Hair.

Then Father asked Mrs. Button and Madame to join us on stage, and when they did, Sister Fabian and Mother Filomina each came out with these bouquets of roses. Red ones. Sister Fabian gave Mrs. Button her bouquet and Madame got hers from Mother Filomina. And Mother Fil not only gave her

her flowers, but then she hugged her for a kind of a long time, and it wasn't one of those fake hugs that people give, but a real one. And when they stopped hugging, Madame blew a kiss to the audience and gave them one of those curtsies like people give to Queen Elizabeth, and one guy even whistled.

And then Father Jerry said, "Well, folks, I guess that wraps things up except for one final detail. So let's all stand and sing, 'God Bless America.'" And everyone did, even me. And in the middle of it, Jackie's lamb started squirming so much that he let him go. Then Eugene let his go, too, and the lambs started running around the stage bleating, and the first and second graders, and even some of us older kids, started chasing them, and one of the lambs jumped off the stage and people in the audience started chasing him, too.

Back up in our classroom, Pauline Papelbon must have been feeling better because I seen her eat some of the refreshments, including two of Ma's pizelles. Zhenya's father kept telling me to have some of his raisin and milk curd strudel, and I didn't really want to but I didn't want to hurt his feelings either, so I tried some. It wasn't that bad, but it wasn't that good either, and when Mr. Kabakov was talking to Marion and his family, I chucked it in the garbage can. I asked Ma where Pop was, and Ma said that it was too bad, but he must not have been able to get away from the lunch counter. "Yes, he did," I said. "I saw him."

"You did? Then I guess he had to go back to the depot and finish up."

While all the other kids and their families were eating and talking and laughing about stuff, I kept looking over at Mr. and Mrs. Twerski and Rosalie.

They were sitting by themselves in the back, looking kinda gloomy. Rosalie had changed back into her regular clothes and had gotten the rest of her beard off, but there was this kind of big red mark on her chin where her goatee had been. When I walked toward her, her eyes squinted like she was getting ready for me to say something snotty. But what I said to her was, "I really liked your play."

"No you didn't," she said. "You told me you thought the ending was dumb." Mrs. Twerski put her hand on Rosalie's arm and shook her head.

"Yeah," I said. "But then I thought about it some more and changed my mind. Now I think it was a good ending."

She blinked. Nodded. "What do you say, sweetie?" Mr. Twerski said.

"Thanks," Rosalie said. I said you're welcome and started to walk away. "Hey, Felix?" she said. When I turned back toward her, she said, "You were a pretty good Jesus, too."

"Yeah?"

"Yeah. Better than that doll, anyway."

"Thanks," I said.

Out in the school parking lot was where Simone and Frances had their disagreement about whether Franz Duzio had only picked his nose or if he had both picked it and eaten it, and Ma said, well, she hadn't seen Franz do either of those things, but maybe that was because she liked to focus on the positive and not always on the negative like *some* people she knew. (She looked at Frances when she said that last part.)

When we got home, there was a note from Pop that said to meet him down at China Village in Easterly so's our family could celebrate what a great job everyone did in the Christmas show, *"especially whoever that kid was who played Baby Jesus. He was terrific!"* To this day, I remember in vivid detail what happened next. . . .

We get in the car—Ma, my sisters, and me—and drive to Easterly. Along the way, I count the number of houses that are decorated with Christmas lights. That song by the Chipmunks, and "White Christmas" and "Jingle Bell Rock" play on the car radio. Plus that French song by the Singing Nun, *"Domenica nica nica. . . ."*

Pop's already there, sitting in a half-circle booth with red plastic upholstery. He's drinking a bottle of beer—Rheingold—and has already ordered Ma this fancy red drink that comes with pineapples and cherries on a stick. "What do you kids want to drink?" he asks us. Me and Frances both want Shirley Temples, and Simone just wants a Coke.

"Ready to order now?" the waitress asks after she brings us our drinks. Pop tells her we need a little more time. I'm still pretty full from all the refreshments in our classroom, but in a few minutes, when the waitress returns (she's wearing a shiny red kimono), I will order a number 16 with gravy, an egg roll, and pork fried rice and eat it all, no doggy bag.

Frances asks Pop for a quarter and, when he fishes one out of his pocket, she gets up and goes over to the jukebox. There's a fish tank right next to it, so I get up, too. There's carp in there, huge ones with bulgy eyes, plus a ceramic mermaid that doesn't have any shirt on. "Woo woo," I go, pointing at the mermaid, and Frances calls me a moron. You get three songs for a quarter. Frances feeds Pop's coin into the machine and punches a bunch of buttons. Dusty Springfield starts singing. *Wishin' and hopin' and thinkin' and prayin' plannin' and dreaming each night of his charms . . .*

After I slide back into the booth, I stick my finger in this orangy stuff in a little dish and taste it. It's good. Sweet. "Duck sauce," Simone says, and I go "Qwack, qwack, qwack." Ma says she'll qwack me if I put my fingers in there again. Then she turns to Pop. "So Felix said you got to the school after all."

And Pop says, "Yeah, right about when that jerky kid threw the bottle cap at the stage and got the bum's rush out of there. When he walked past me, I felt like getting up and giving him a good, swift kick in the *culo* for good measure." Ma asks him, did he have to go back and close up the lunch counter? Was that why we didn't see him up in my classroom for the refreshments?

"Nope," he says. "That wasn't it." He's smiling kinda mysterious, like that time when, for Mother's Day, he bought Ma a dishwasher and hid it under some old blankets in our garage.

"Where were you then, Poppy?" Frances asks.

"Do you want me to tell you or should I *show* you?" Pop says. And we all go *huh?* Then he reaches down on the floor, picks up this big envelope, takes out three glossy black and white photos, and hands one to each of us kids.

Simone's says, "For Simone, With my fondest wishes, Cousin Annette."

Frances's says, "For Frances, With my fondest wishes, Cousin Annette."

And mine says, "For Felix, Who was the best performer in the whole Christmas show!! Love, Cousin Annette."

Pop asks me if, when I waved at him from the stage, did I see that both him and Annette were waving back? And I go, "That big-hair lady was *her*?"

"Sure was, kiddo. Her father called me. She's in the middle of a press tour for her new movie. She'd just left Manhattan and was heading up to Boston, but I didn't want to say anything because she wasn't sure she'd have time to stop on her way and I didn't want you kids to be disappointed. What a sweet gal she is—as sweet as sugar. And man oh man, you should've seen the limo she was riding in. First class all the way. . . . Simone, honey, maybe you better close your mouth now, or you're going to start catching flies in there."

"She was actually *there?*" Simone says. "In the same auditorium *we* were? You're not just kidding us?"

Pop asks, what does she think? That *he* autographed those pictures?

"But for real, Pop? She was really, really there?"

I tell Simone yes, she was. Because other than Pop, I was the only one in our whole family who saw her.

"Until now," Pop says. He's looking toward the front of the restaurant, and when I look, too, there's this big black limousine pulling up to the curb. The waitress returns. "Ready to order now?" she asks. "Everyone here?"

"Almost," Pop says.

The front door opens, and there she is. Pop stands, calls her name, and waves. She waves back, smiling, and starts toward us.

Epilogue

Sister M. Dymphna (*née* Jean McGannon) returned to her Saint Aloysius Gonzaga fifth graders in January of 1965, at which time she halted the teaching of conversational French but also discontinued her policy of ranking pupils academically on the blackboard and by seating chart. In 1980, she was diagnosed with bipolar disorder (then called manic-depressive disorder) and responded well to treatment. In 1984, her order forsook traditional nuns' habits for street-clothes and launched a number of social justice initiatives. Today, seventy-nine years old, Sister Jean volunteers at Ecole Agape, a school for impoverished Haitian girls.

Father Gerald "Jerry" Hanrahan left the priesthood to marry in 1967. A retired social worker, Hanrahan lives with his family in Seattle, Washington.

In 1968, **Monsignor Angus Muldoon** succumbed to emphysema and alcohol-related diabetes. In his honor, St. Aloysius Gonzaga Parochial School's advisory board established the Monsignor Muldoon Memorial Medallion, an award given each year to a graduating eighth grade boy who exhibits, in the manner of the school's namesake, "high moral conduct." In 1968, the inaugural prize was shared by **Roland** and **Ronald Kubiak.**

Mother M. Filomina (*née* Phyllis Benvenuto) left her post as principal of St. Aloysius G in 1979 to become the residential supervisor of the Holy Family

Home, a shelter for the homeless in Worcester, Massachusetts. She held that position until her death in 1986.

Following the retirement of her husband, a haberdasher, **Madame Marguerite Frechette** returned to her native Québec. Active in community theater there ever since, she has directed and/or performed in no fewer than seventy-seven productions. The Frechettes, now in their mid-eighties, visit Paris yearly.

Pauline Papelbon and her sister were withdrawn from St. Aloysius Gonzaga in March of 1965 and sent to live with out-of-state relatives. Under Sister Dymphna's direction, Pauline's former classmates wrote and signed a group letter to her, but she never wrote back. Recently, however, she resurfaced on the *Dr. Phil Show* in a program titled "Love Your Life, Not Your Carbs."

As a district manager for the Dunkin' Donuts corporation, **Franz Duzio** oversees the operation of more than 200 stores in central and western Massachusetts. The former lead singer of the Skinnydippers, a surf band, he is also a published poet whose work has appeared in the literary magazines *Upwind*, *The Boll Weevil Review*, and *Art & Noise*. With his son, Franz Duzio, Jr., he edits *Screw You: An On-Line 'Zine of the Arts*. Duzio and his wife (the former **Geraldine Balchunas**) have five children and one grandchild, Franz Duzio III.

Marion Pemberton borrowed his signature line—"Wait'll the NAACP hears about this!"—from entertainer Sammy Davis, Jr. At the 1964 Academy Awards telecast (at which Sidney Poitier became the first black American to win the "best actor" Oscar), Davis, a presenter, was handed the wrong envelope. His ad-lib received the best laugh of the evening. In March of 1965 Marion Pemberton's oldest sister, Brenda, a college student, was injured and imprisoned during the Selma-to-Montgomery march, and Pemberton identifies this as a defining event in his life. A graduate of the University of Pennsylvania School of Law, he is a Southern Poverty Law Center attorney. He and his wife, a pediatrician, live in Marietta, Georgia, where they organized campaign fundraisers for Barack Obama in 2008. Having dropped the "n" in his given name, he is now known as Mario Pemberton, Attorney at Law.

Following the fall of the Soviet government in 1991, a front page *New London Day* article recounted the 1963 defection to the U.S. via Norway of Boris Kabakov, a writer and KGB infiltrator, his wife Lina Kabakova, an industrial engineer, and their niece, **Evgeniya "Zhenya" Kabakova,** who was passed off as the couple's daughter for security reasons. The daughter of itinerant circus performers, Zhenya Kabakova had been orphaned at the age of ten when her father, Ivan Kabakov, Boris Kabakov's brother, was killed by a spooked elephant during a thunderstorm. (Ivan Kabakov's wife had predeceased him.) Following her graduation from St. Aloysius

Gonzaga and the Academy of the Sacred Blood, a Catholic girls' school, where her peers voted her Class Dancer, Class Clown, and "Most Boy Crazy," she entered the Zachary Smith Academy of Beauty and became a licensed hairdresser. Married and divorced twice, she has over 800 "friends" on the Facebook social network and is today employed as a blackjack dealer at Circus, Circus in Las Vegas, Nevada.

Thrice married and divorced, **Lonny Flood** is a graduate of Windham (CT) Technical High School. Employed by a number of area plumbing businesses, he received his foreman's license in 1996 and oversaw the plumbing operation of Wequonnoc Moon Casino and Resort, retiring from that position in 2008. He owns time-shares in Sandwich, Massachusetts, and Branson, Missouri, and, through Facebook, has reconnected with his former classmate, Zhenya Kabakova. Recently treated for high blood pressure and erectile dysfunction, Flood takes a daily diuretic and

Viagra as needed. He is in the process of relocating to Las Vegas, Nevada.

Rosalie Twerski was valedictorian of her classes at both St. Aloysius Gonzaga and the Academy of the Sacred Blood. A *magna cum laude* graduate of Notre Dame University's School of Business, she subsequently toured for two seasons with Up With People! Married to James Hibbard, an actuary, hers is a familiar face seen on billboard and grocery cart advertising across east-of-the-river Connecticut, from which she declares, "Take it from me, Rose Twerski-Hibbard, Re/Max Realtors' Top Seller Month After Month After Month: IF I CAN'T SELL YOUR HOUSE IN 60 DAYS, I'LL BUY IT MYSELF!"

Alvin "Chino" Molinaro purchased the New London Bus Station's lunch counter from its previous owners in 1985. The business went into foreclosure the following year, after which time Molinaro relocated to

Orlando, Florida, where, when last heard from, he was employed by KleenPoolz, a swimming pool maintenance company.

Following his retirement from the food service business, **Salvatore "Sal" Funicello** was active in Festa Italiana, an annual community event, and was the New London County Senior Citizens' bocce champion for six consecutive years. Surrounded by his three children, he succumbed to congestive heart failure in 2001. His final words were, "Take care, kiddos. I'm running out of gas. God bless."

In retirement, **Marie (Napolitano) Funicello** was active in the St. Aloysius Gonzaga Rosary Society and the church's Grief Committee, for which she knitted "comfort shawls" for deceased parishioners' loved ones and cooked for post-funeral buffets. A victim of stroke-related dementia in her last years, she resided at Easterly, Rhode Island's Saint Catherine of Genoa Nursing Home. In October of 2005, she informed her son Felix that her husband Sal had dropped by that morning to help her pack. Rather than pointing out that Sal had been dead for over four years, Felix asked her if she was going on a trip, to which she replied, with a Cheshire grin, "As if you didn't know." She died in her sleep that evening.

Perhaps it was her playpen encounter with her later-to-be-famous third cousin at a family picnic that made **Simone Funicello** long for an Annette-like life. (At the age of eleven, she had begged her parents for permission to have her name legally changed to *Jeannette* Funicello.) As a stepping stone to her own imagined Hollywood career, Simone enrolled in modeling school in 1966. Her modeling jobs were few: a Grange fashion show, a weekend stint as a Chicken of the Sea mermaid positioned in a papier-mâché scallop shell at a Hartford, Connecticut, food show. In 1967, she entered the Miss New London County beauty pageant but failed to place in the pageant's top five. She entered dental hygienist school soon after. For the past twenty-four years, she has been employed by the office of Maya Paulous, D.D.S. She resides in Niantic, Connecticut, with her husband of twenty-nine years, Jeffrey Sands, and the couple's son, Luke. As do no fewer than four other family members on his mother's side, Luke Sands, twenty-seven, lives with the challenges of multiple sclerosis.

In the living room of her Noank, Connecticut, home, **Frances Funicello** displays a framed 1966 photograph of herself, a bubble-haired radio contest winner, standing shoulder to shoulder with her blond, bubble-haired idol, British pop star Dusty Springfield. Frances earned a Bachelor's degree in early childhood education from the University of Connecticut and a Master's degree in reading from New York University. She is employed as a reading specialist in the Stonington, Connecticut, school system. Like Dusty Springfield, Frances came out as a lesbian in the mid-1980s. "Just a phase," her mother assured her father, but Frances's parents came to love their daughter's partner, Victoria Jankowski, a U.S. Navy nurse who in 1996 ran afoul of the U.S. military's "Don't Ask, Don't Tell" policy. Frances and Victoria were married in February of 2009, shortly after gay marriage was legalized in Connecticut. The couple enjoys hiking with their two dogs, Ella and Libby.

During his freshman year at Alexander Hamilton Senior High School, **Felix Funicello** grew five inches and finally became taller than over 50 percent of the girls in his class. The subsequent elongation of his face and the soft, dark down that had begun sprouting above his top lip made him look less Dondi-like. At Hamilton High, he took honors courses, ran cross country and track, and was elected class treasurer. An English major at the University of Massachusetts, he unexpectedly fell in love with film—*Midnight Cowboy, Fellini Satyricon, Five Easy Pieces, The Last Picture Show.* In his senior year, he opted for graduate school, wanting both to study movies more widely and deeply, but also to escape his parents' never-quite-spoken fantasy that he would return to New London and run the lunch counter with, and then for, them. He met his future wife, Katherine Schulman, at the Waverly Theatre, a cramped fifty-seat alternative movie house in Easterly, Rhode Island, that featured stale popcorn, sticky floors, and an excellent Tuesday night foreign film series that Schulman organized. It was at the Waverly that Felix became enamored not only of Kat but also of the French film directors Truffaut, Godard, and Malle, whose work he analyzed in his doctoral thesis, which was later published by a small arts press. In 1983, the year the couple married, Kat gave birth to their daughter, Aliza, and Felix was hired as an assistant professor of film studies at Emerson College. Kat and Felix divorced in 1991. To date, Dr. Funicello has published six books on film and is currently at work on a seventh: an examination of the second half of actress Bette Davis's career, from the 1950s *All About Eve* through *Whatever Happened to Baby Jane?*, *Hush . . . Hush, Sweet Charlotte*, and the films of her final years. After his parents' deaths,

Felix wanted nothing of theirs except the family photographs, of which he was made unofficial curator. Of those hundreds and hundreds of black and white, Polaroid, Kodachrome, Instamatic, 35 mm, and digital photos, Felix has three favorites, each taken in 1964: a picture of his mother posed between TV personality Art Linkletter and future U.S. President Ronald Reagan; a photo of his family at their New London bus station food concession, Felix and his sisters seated on stools in the foreground, his parents standing behind the lunch counter; and a snapshot taken by a waitress at a Chinese restaurant. In this picture, Simone and Frances flank their cousin Annette on the left, Felix and his parents on the right. Everyone smiles and waves.

Born in Utica, New York, **Annette Funicello** was cast by Walt Disney as one of TV's original Mouseketeers in 1955 and quickly became the most popular cast member of the *Mickey Mouse Club*. She also starred in a number of Disney motion pictures and recorded four Billboard chart hits. With her co-star Frankie Avalon, she later became a beach picture icon. In 1965, she married agent Jack Gilardi and the couple had three children together, Gina, Jack, and Jason. Later divorced from Gilardi, she married Glen Holt in 1986. In 1992, she was designated a Disney Legend. That same year, she disclosed to the public that she had been diagnosed with multiple sclerosis. The following year, she established the California Community Foundation's Annette Funicello Fund for Neurological Disorders. Blind, wheelchair-bound, and in the advanced stages of her debilitating disease, to many of her baby boomer fans she remains America's Italian-American sweetheart.

Acknowledgments

Thanks to Harper's publisher, Jonathan Burnham, and my good friend, Barbara Dombrowski, who, coincidentally, on the very same day in January of 2009, both suggested that I write a Christmas story. Nah, I thought. But the next day, I concocted the name Felix Funicello and was off and running.

A writer does his best, then passes off his work to those professionals who edit, design, publicize, vet, sell, and send a finished book into the world. I'm ever-grateful to my editor, Terry Karten, and my agent, Kassie Evashevski, both of whom encouraged me, laughed at the funny stuff, and nudged me toward making this a better book. Thanks as well to the crackerjack Harper team, especially Christina Bailly, Leslie Cohen, Beth Silfin, Tina Andreadis, Kathy Schneider, Archie Ferguson, Leah Carlson-Stanisic, Lydia Weaver, Jennifer Daddio, and Evie Righter. And once again, a tip of the hat to the HarperCollins sales force, the best in the business.

One of my oldest and best buddies, Bob Parzych, had vivid recall of his mother's trip to California when her "Sweet Dreams Cream Torte" made her a state finalist in the 1959 Pillsbury Bake-Off. Another good friend, Harry Mantzaris, shared his recollections of the days when his family ran the lunch counter at the old New London, Connecticut, bus station. Bob's and Harry's memories provided the springboard from which I plunged into this tale.

Thanks to the following writers and readers who looked at and listened to the various drafts of this story and offered me the gift of their critical feedback:

Doug Anderson, Bruce Cohen, Steve Dauer, John Ekizian, Careen Jennings, Leslie Johnson, Terese Karmel, Chris Lamb, Justin Lamb, Sari Rosenblatt, and Ellen Zahl. Special thanks to Pam Lewis, who helped me solve the dilemma of the novel's epilogue chapter. (Pam and I have been friends for 25+ years, since the days when we were students in the Vermont College MFA in Writing program.) Special thanks as well to Aaron Bremyer, my loyal, longstanding, and soon-to-depart office assistant, who listened to these chapters first and laughed the hardest. Good luck, Aaron.

Thanks to the many friends and acquaintances who shared their humorous recollections of parochial school, especially Kathy Wyatt, whose memory of a former classmate kick-started my creation of Zhenya Kabakova. And speaking of Zhenya, thanks to the following who helped me with that character's saucy Russian vernacular: Lukas Casey, Ludmila Casey, Svetlana Lyubisheva, Dima Nigmatulin, and Sveta Nigmatulina. Thanks, too, to Terry Karten for correcting my high school French. Speaking of which, *merci bien* to Irène Rose, my high school French teacher of some forty years ago, who bears no resemblance to the novel's flamboyant Madame Frechette but whose positive influence endures.

This novel was fueled by golden crispy shrimp, moo shu chicken, black bean soup, and enchiladas suiza. My thanks to the cooks, servers, and hosts at Mansfield, Connecticut's Coyote Flaco and Chang's Garden restaurants, where our writers group meetings are often held.

Finally, a salute to entertainers Annette Funicello, Brenda Lee, and the late, great Dusty Springfield; to songwriters Burt Bacharach and Hal David ("Wishin' and Hopin'"), Richard and Robert Sherman ("Tall Paul"), and Johnny Marks ("Rockin' Around the Christmas Tree"); to cartoonists Gus Edson, Irwin Hasen, and later Bob Oksner (*Dondi*); and to Orville "Andy" Andrews (a.k.a. Ranger Andy), host of *The Ranger Station*, a live children's program on what was then WTIC-TV and is now WFSB-Channel

3, a CBS affiliate. As a Cub Scout, I did, in fact, visit the Ranger Station when I was about Felix's age. But though local legend has it that Felix's inappropriate joke did indeed get told on the air, it wasn't I who told it. Scout's honor.

Suggestion for charitable giving

Readers who wish to donate to the National Multiple Sclerosis Society in honor of Annette Funicello or others afflicted with MS may do so in these three ways:

- By website: http://www.nationalmssociety.org/wally lamb
- By mail: National MS Society, P.O. Box 4527, New York, NY 10163
- By phone: 1.800.344.4867